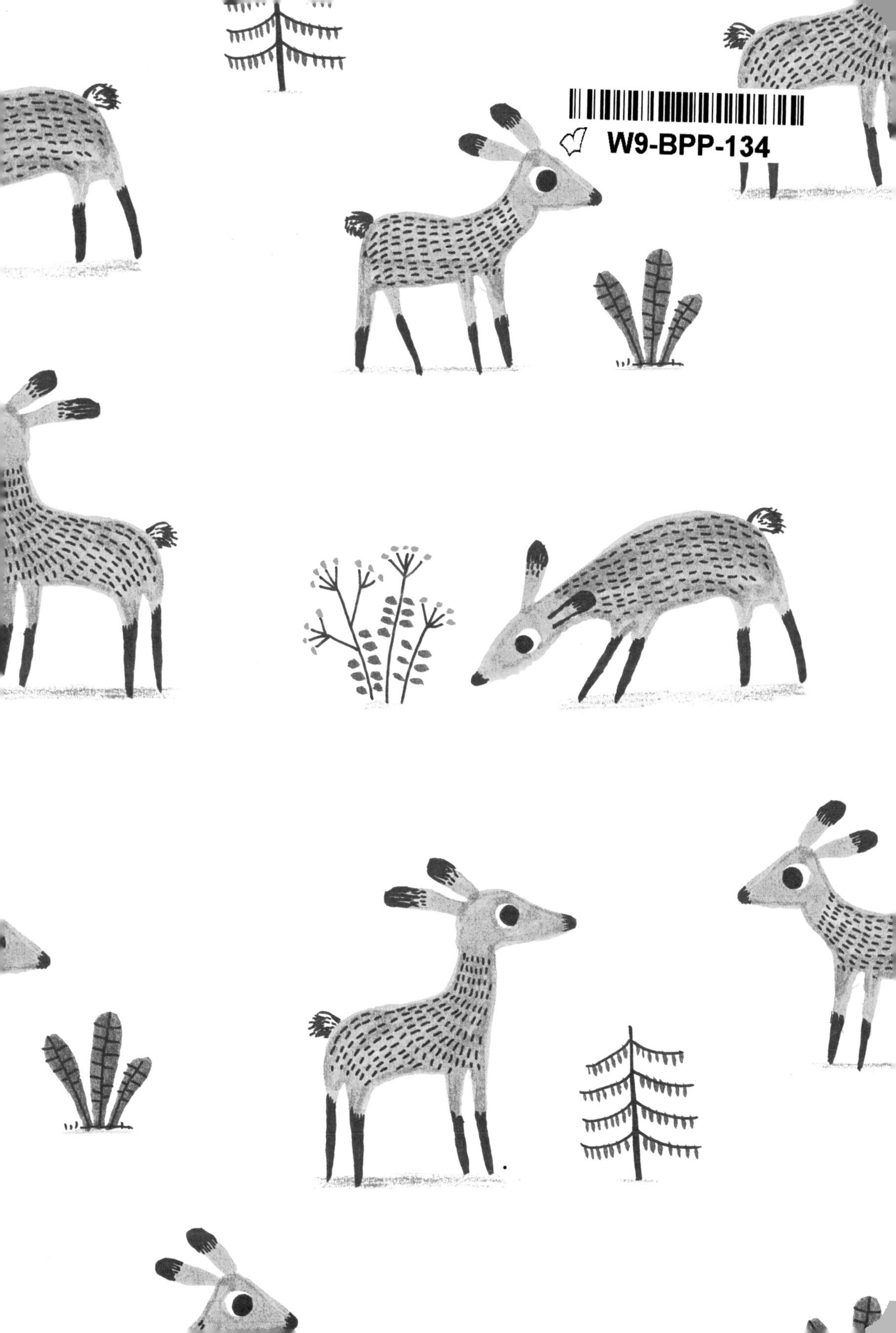

3 1526 050228417

iF FOUND

PLEASE RETURN TO

ELiSE GRAVEL

★ ★ ★ ★ ★

Translated by Shira Adriance

ENFANT

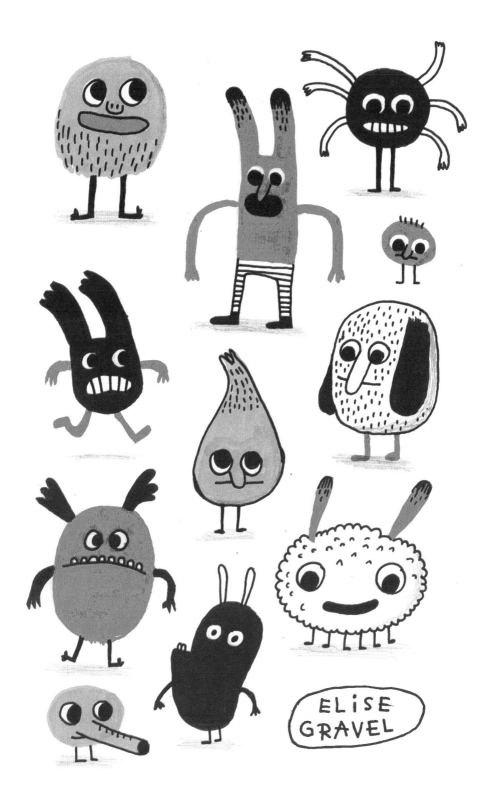

ELISE
GRAVEL

At night, when my daughters are asleep,
i draw in my black notebook. I draw complete
nonsense. Whatever comes to my mind.
With markers, gouache, watercolour, lead
pencils, or just ordinary pens. Even with
my kids' pencils.

When I draw in my black notebook, it feels
good—it's as if I let out all the ideas that
are bouncing around in my head. Ridiculous
ideas, crazy ideas, bizarre ideas.

I never critique the drawings in my black
notebook. I give myself the right to fail,
to mess up, to create ugly drawings.
I'm kind to myself. In my notebook,
i do what i want.

In the morning, my daughters come
peek at the new drawings and laugh.
They give me new ideas.

COMPLETE NONSENSE

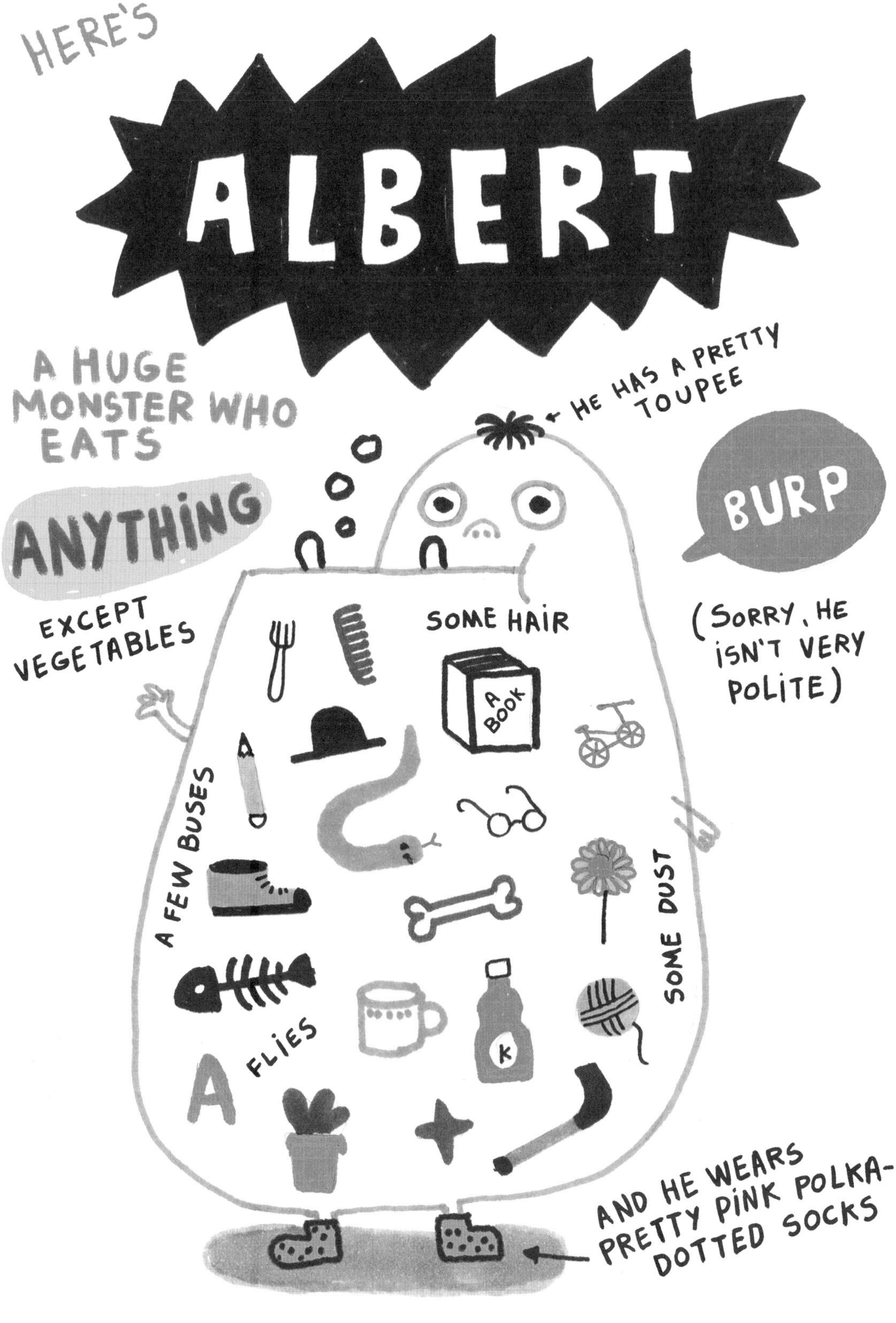
HERE'S
ALBERT
A HUGE MONSTER WHO EATS
ANYTHING
EXCEPT VEGETABLES
HE HAS A PRETTY TOUPEE
BURP
(SORRY, HE ISN'T VERY POLITE)
SOME HAIR
A BOOK
A FEW BUSES
SOME DUST
FLIES
A
K
AND HE WEARS PRETTY PINK POLKA-DOTTED SOCKS

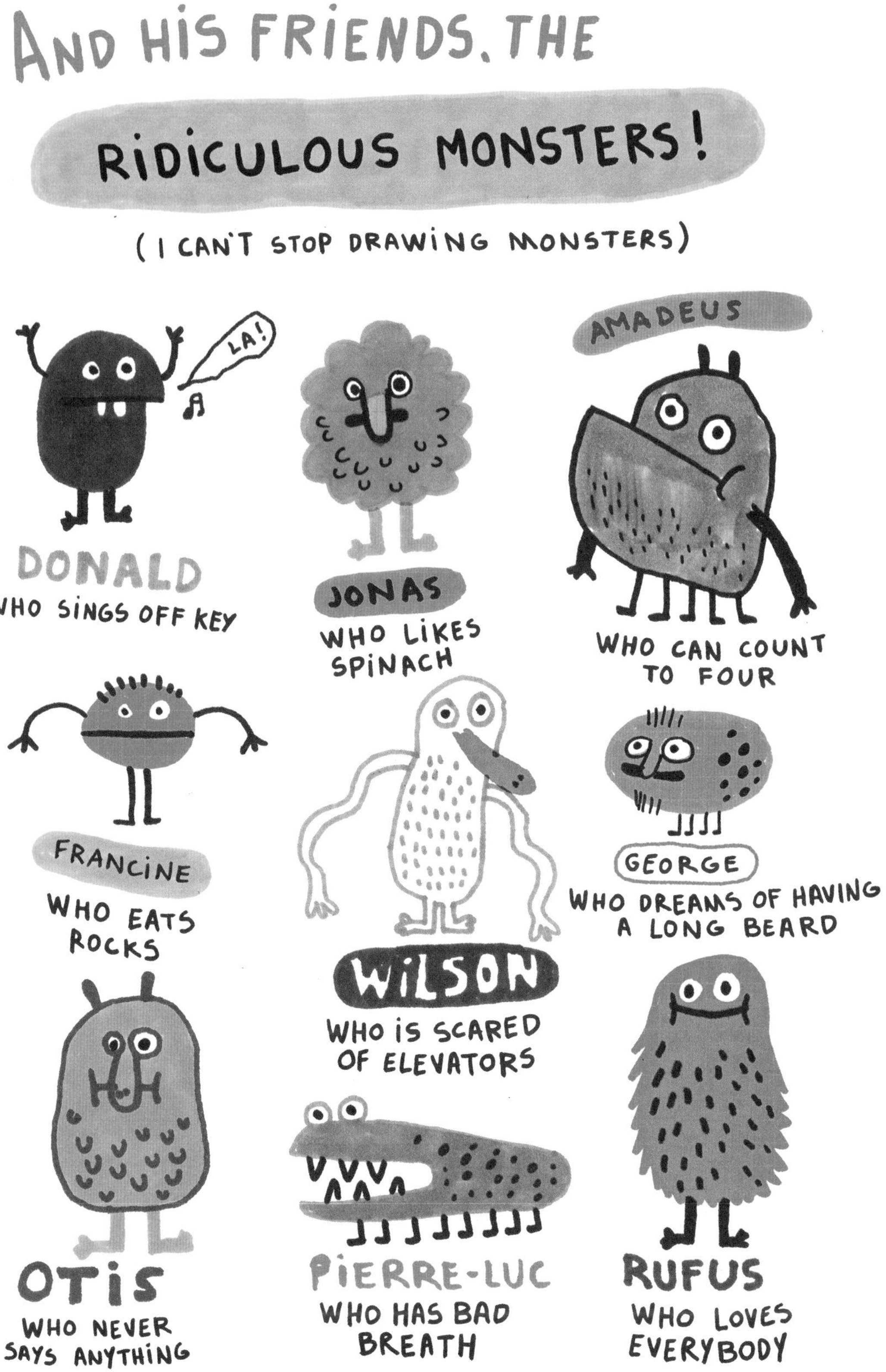
AND HIS FRIENDS, THE
RIDICULOUS MONSTERS!
(I CAN'T STOP DRAWING MONSTERS)
LA!
DONALD
WHO SINGS OFF KEY
JONAS
WHO LIKES SPINACH
AMADEUS
WHO CAN COUNT TO FOUR
FRANCINE
WHO EATS ROCKS
WILSON
WHO IS SCARED OF ELEVATORS
GEORGE
WHO DREAMS OF HAVING A LONG BEARD
OTIS
WHO NEVER SAYS ANYTHING
PIERRE-LUC
WHO HAS BAD BREATH
RUFUS
WHO LOVES EVERYBODY

MY WEIRD GARDEN

WITH:

LOLA The carnivorous VEGETARIAN plant

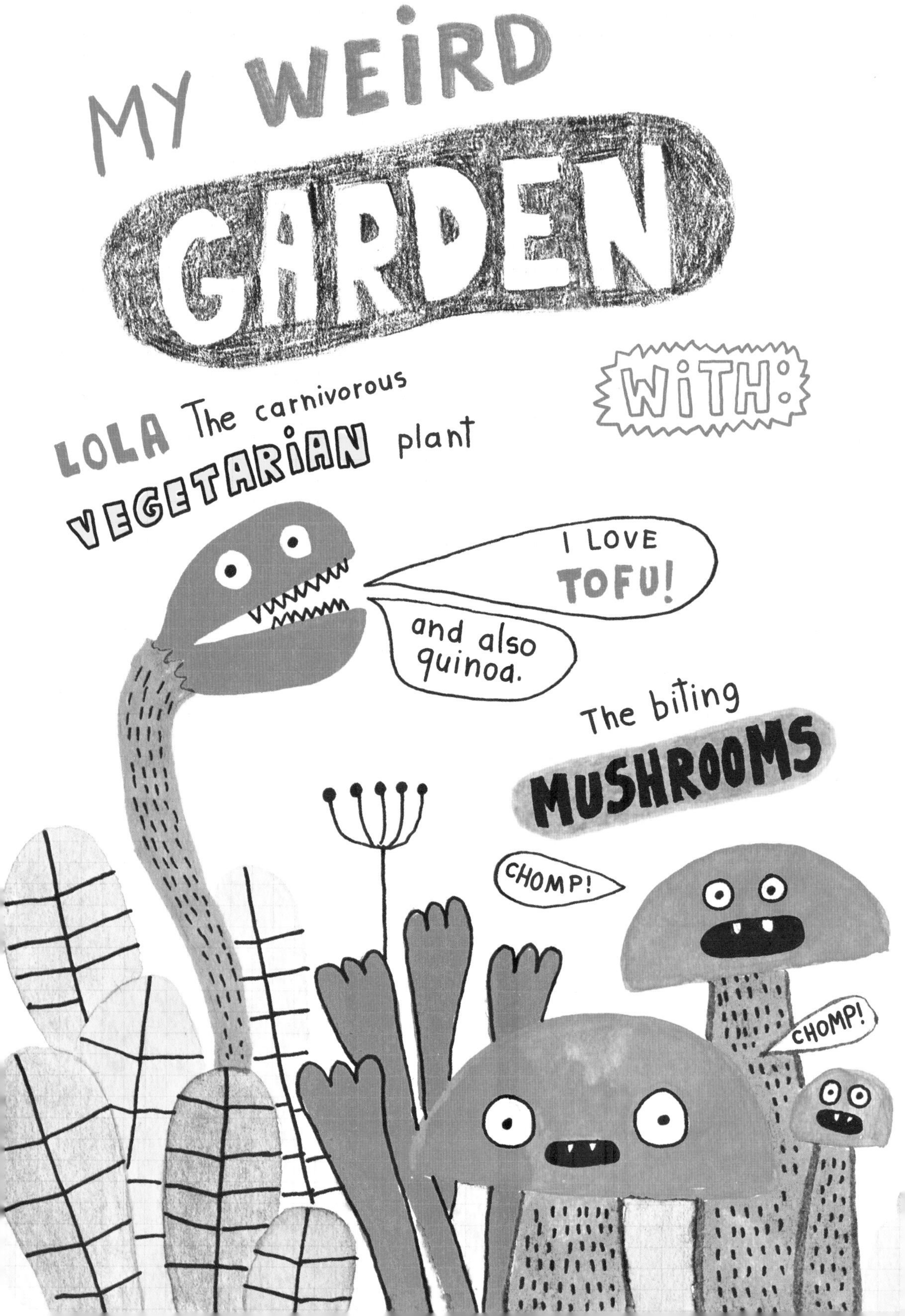

I LOVE TOFU!
and also quinoa.
The biting MUSHROOMS
CHOMP!
CHOMP!

The little flowers who talk
all the time
And then he said, "move aside."
i'll tell you about my dream.
I don't like onions or tomatoes, personally.
The Feet plants
The BEATLES FLOWERS
YEAH!
YEAH!

Bubba

THE BEAR

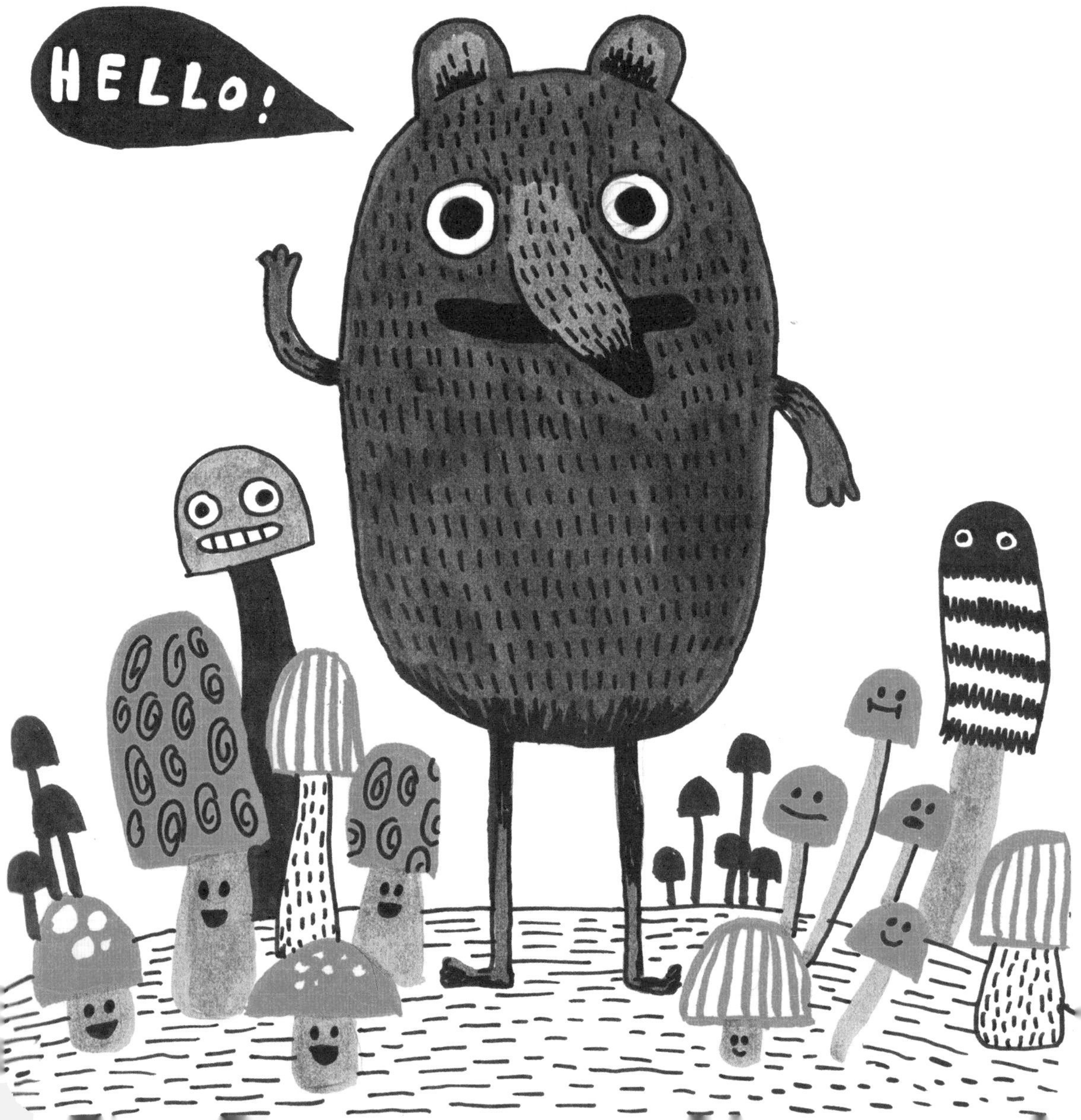
HELLO!

There are caves in the forest near my cottage.
Lots of caves, set in a rock cliff.
And in the caves, there are bears.

I've never seen any, but I know
they're there. I know there's at least one
because my daughters and I saw bear
poo on the path. Huge poops! As big
as your shoes. With blueberries in them.
I'm telling you, they were so big, there's
no way they were rabbit poops.
Or maybe it was a big rabbit.

In my head, I call this bear that I've never
seen Bubba. I'm sure he's nice and that he,
like me, enjoys hunting for mushrooms.

I hope to see him for real one day.
But from far away. Really, really far.

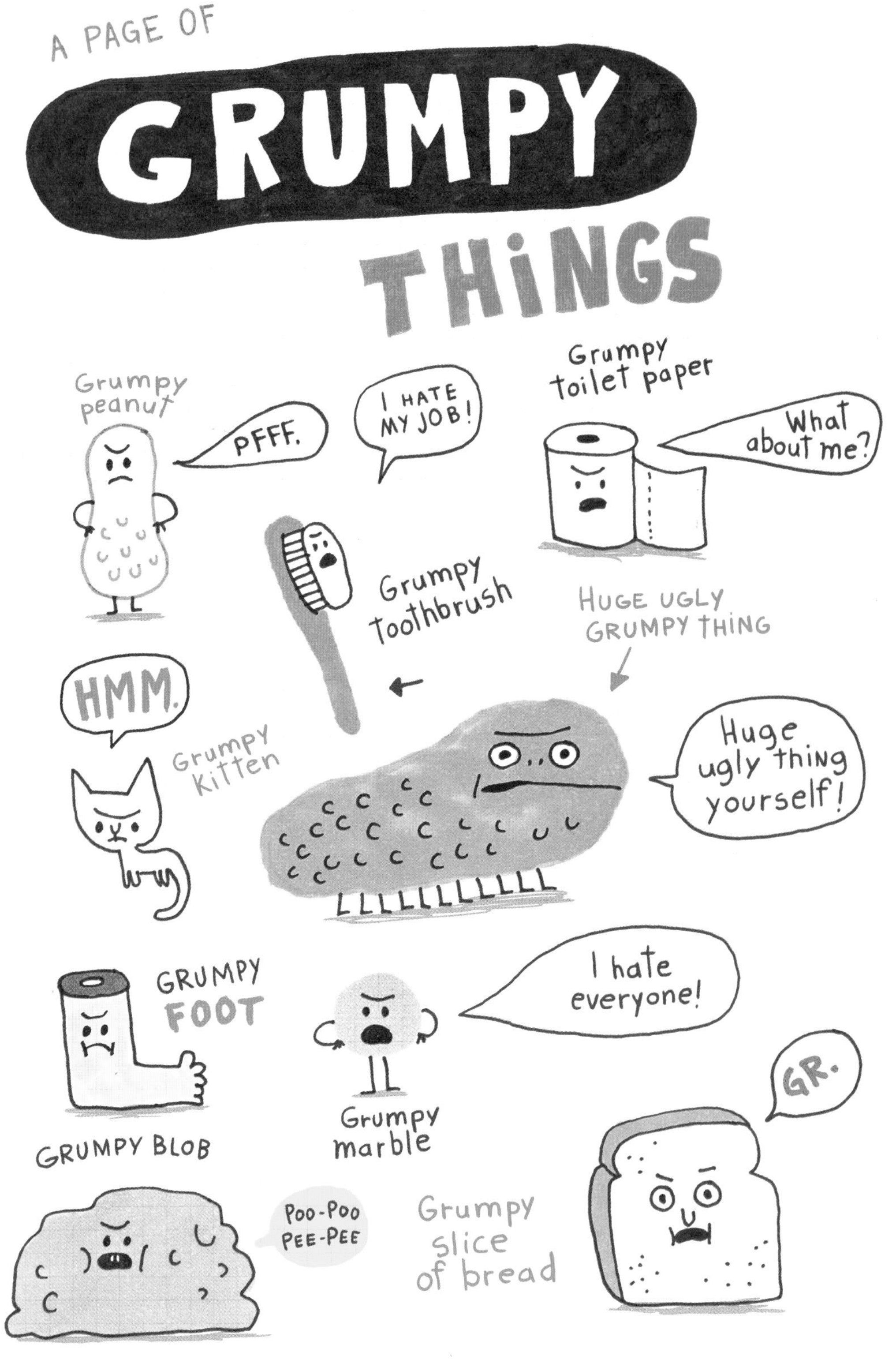

A PAGE OF
GRUMPY
THiNGS
Grumpy peanut
PFFF.
I HATE MY JOB!
Grumpy toilet paper
What about me?
Grumpy Toothbrush
HUGE UGLY GRUMPY THING
HMM.
Grumpy Kitten
Huge ugly thing yourself!
GRUMPY FOOT
I hate everyone!
GR.
GRUMPY BLOB
Grumpy marble
Poo-Poo PEE-PEE
Grumpy slice of bread

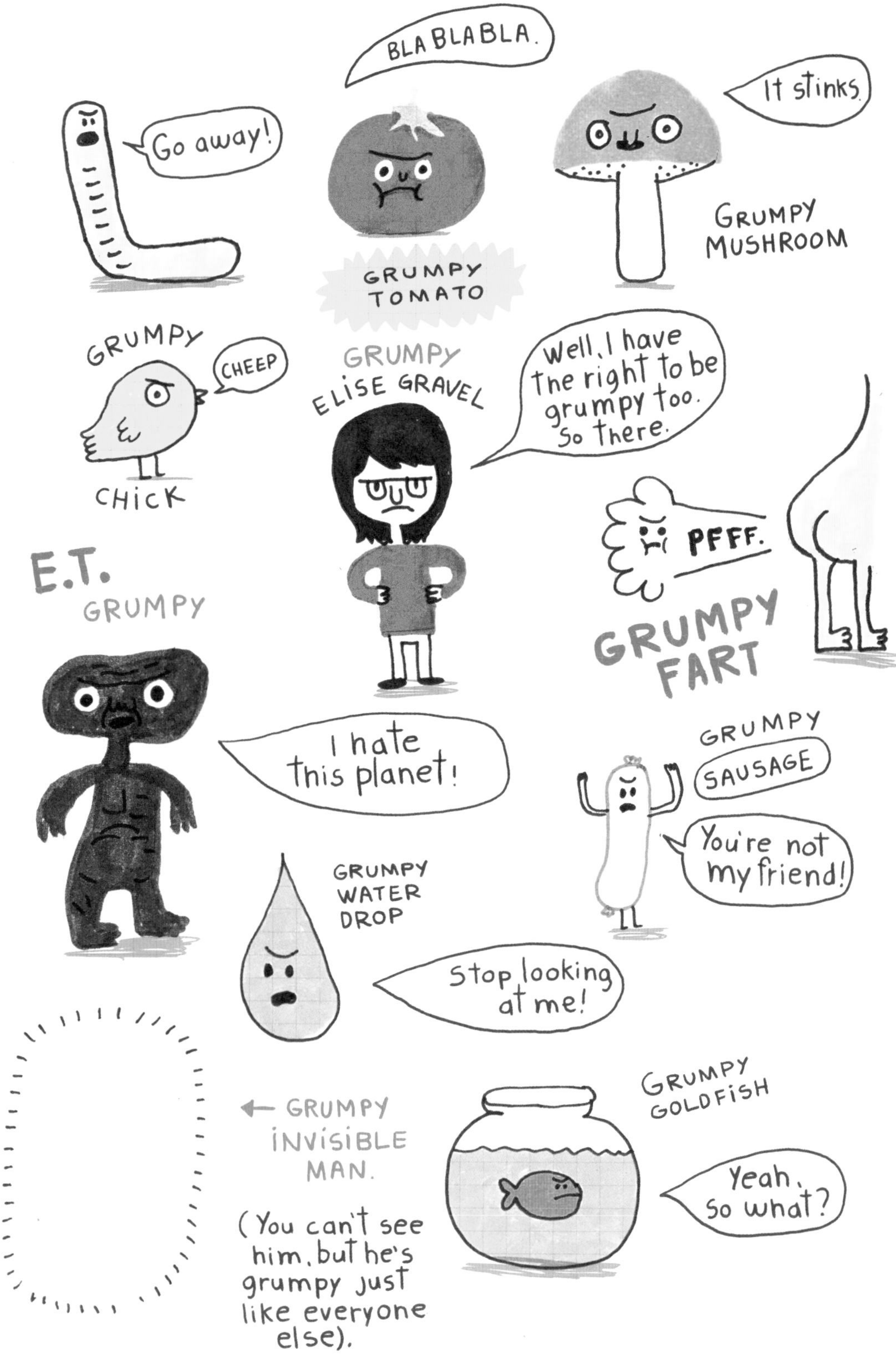

Go away!
BLA BLA BLA.
GRUMPY TOMATO
It stinks.
GRUMPY MUSHROOM
GRUMPY CHICK
CHEEP
GRUMPY ELISE GRAVEL
Well, I have the right to be grumpy too. So there.
PFFF.
GRUMPY FART
E.T. GRUMPY
I hate this planet!
GRUMPY SAUSAGE
You're not my friend!
GRUMPY WATER DROP
Stop looking at me!
← GRUMPY INVISIBLE MAN.
(You can't see him, but he's grumpy just like everyone else).
GRUMPY GOLDFISH
Yeah, so what?

MY IMAGINARY FRIENDS

When i was young, i had three imaginary friends. They were these little flying guys who played with me in the back alley when there was no one else around.

Today, i'm grown up, but my brain continues to produce imaginary friends nonstop. I draw them everywhere: in my books, on little scraps of paper, on place mats in restaurants.

If you need an imaginary friend, help yourself. Take whichever one you want. They're all nice and friendly. Consider them a gift.

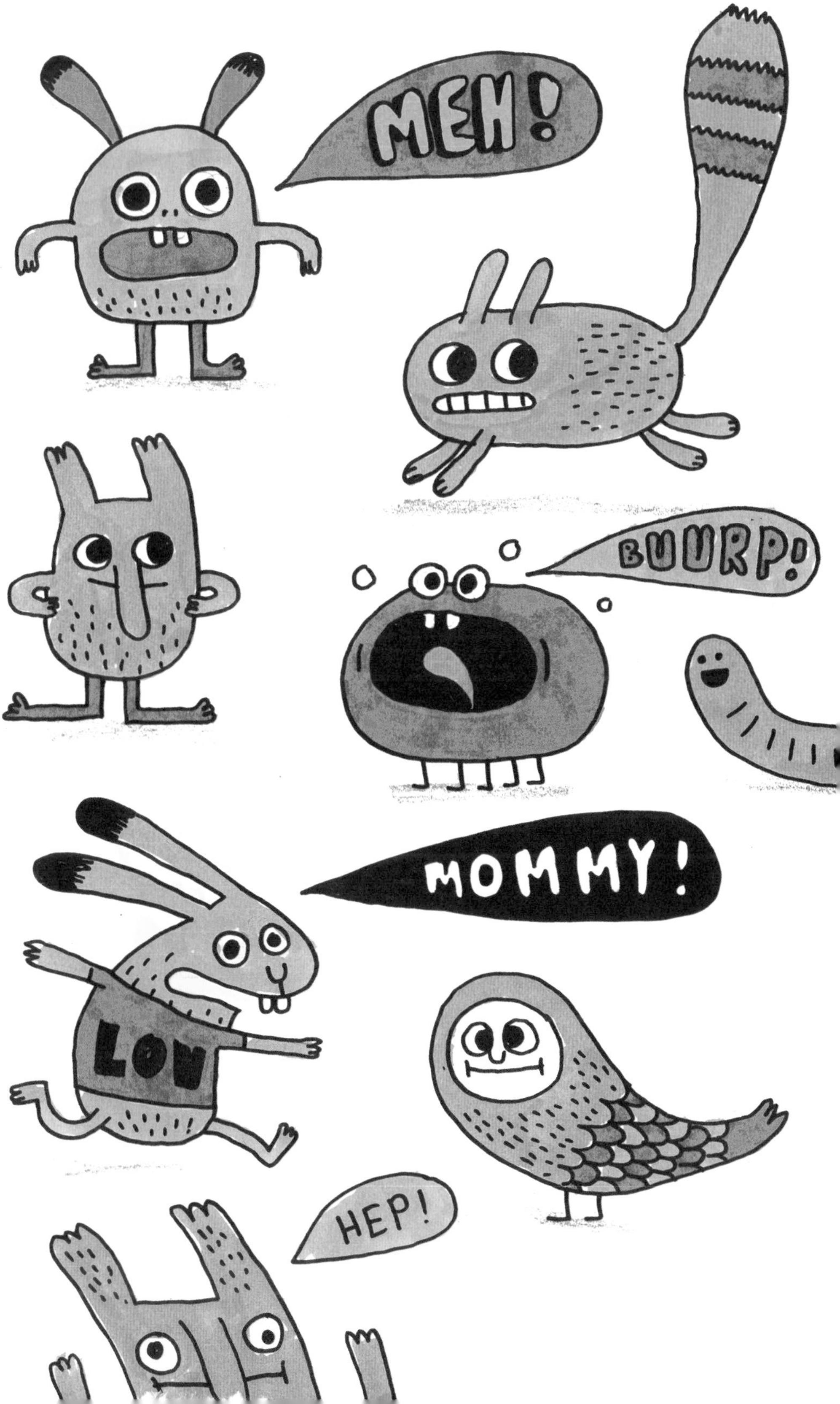
MEH!
BUURP!
MOMMY!
LOV
HEP!

THE SPECKLED PEPPERPOP

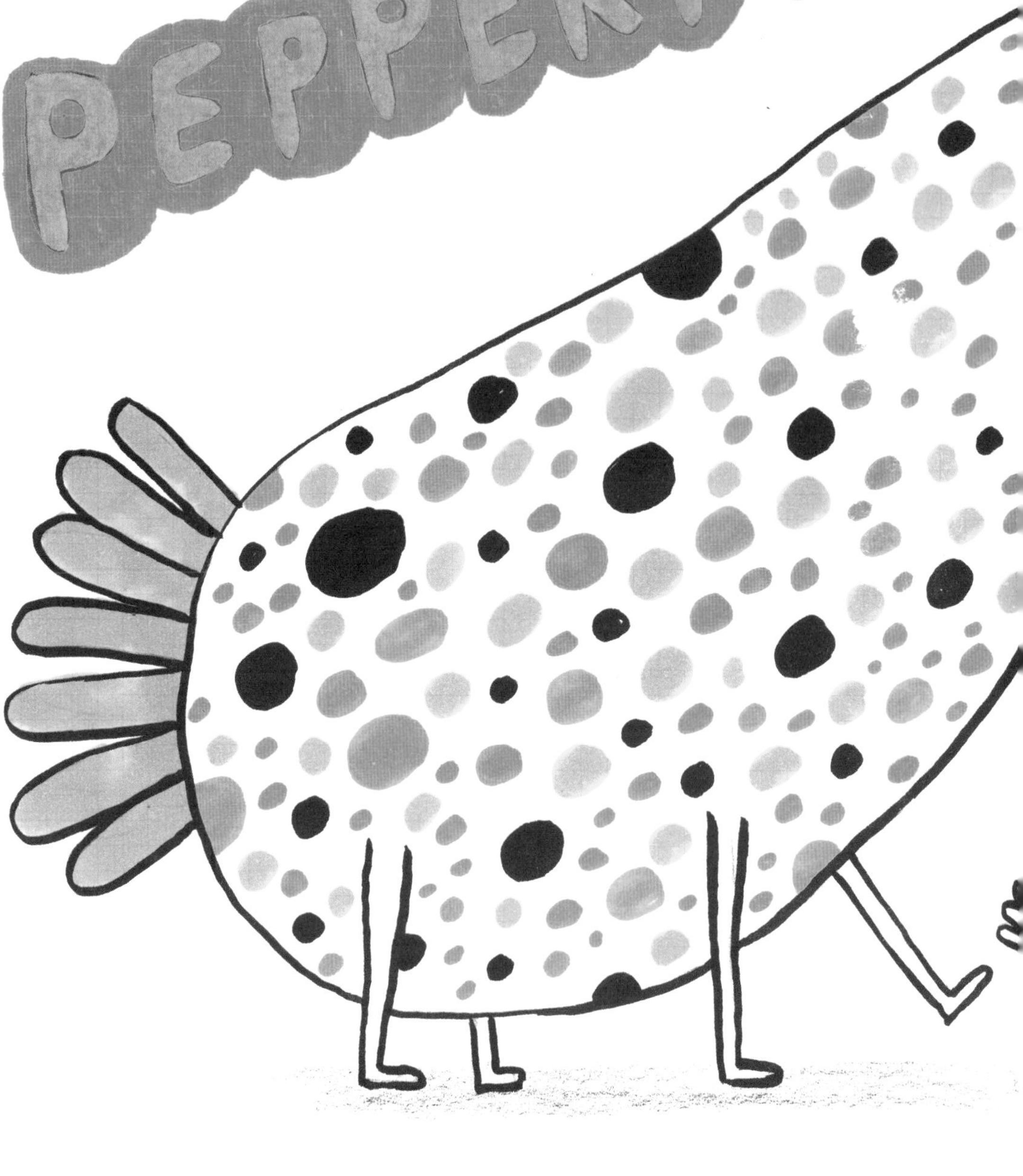

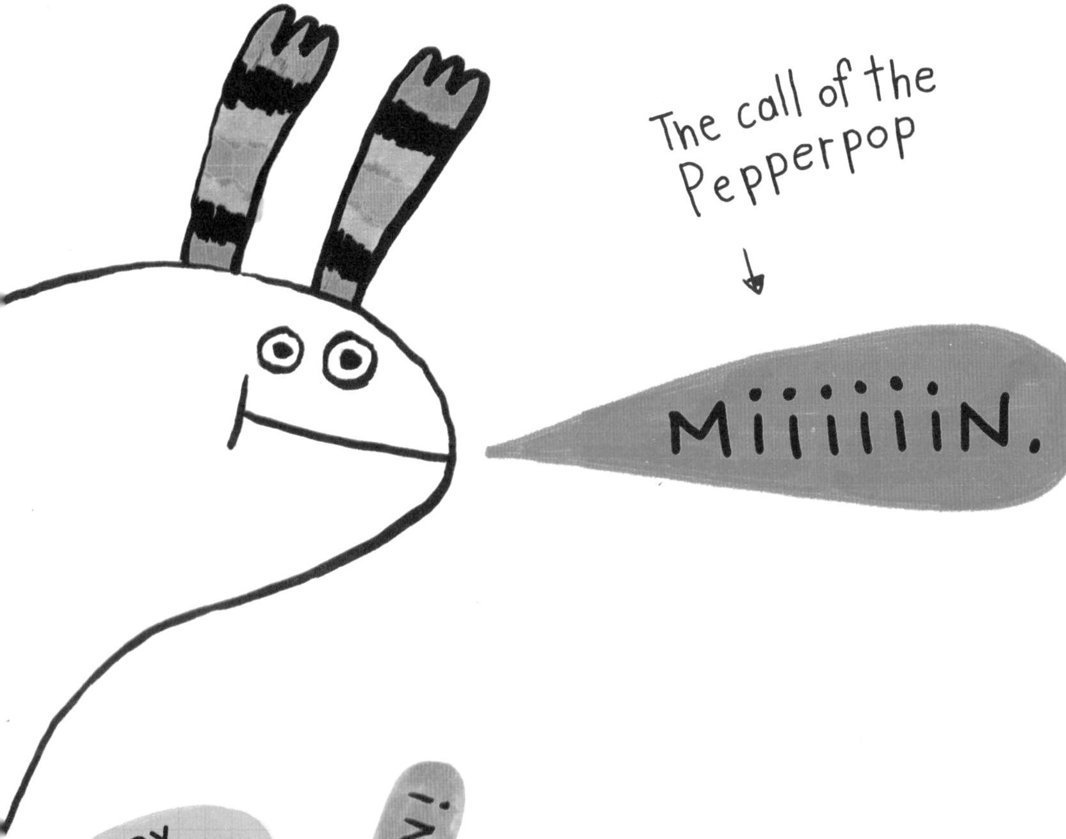
The call of the Pepperpop
MiiiiiN.

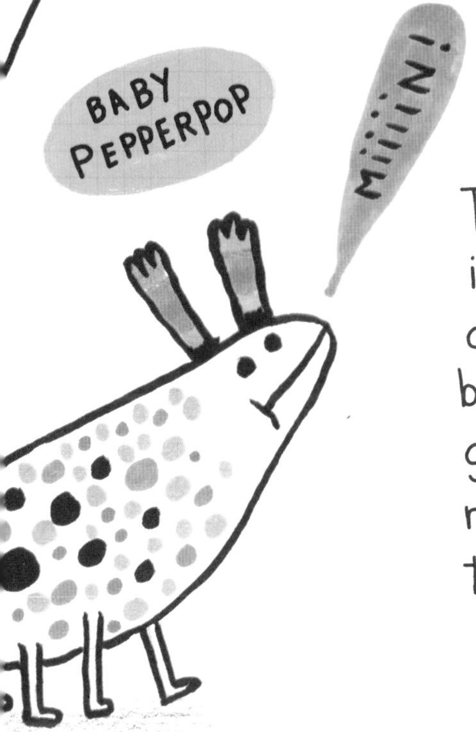
BABY PEPPERPOP
MiiiiiN!

The speckled pepperpop lives in holes in the green prairies out west. They feed on daisy buds and cow dung. They're gentle and timid, but they really like it when tourists take their photos.

THE **MICROBE** PAGE

Bacteria are really fun to draw, because you can draw almost anything, kind of like when you draw monsters.

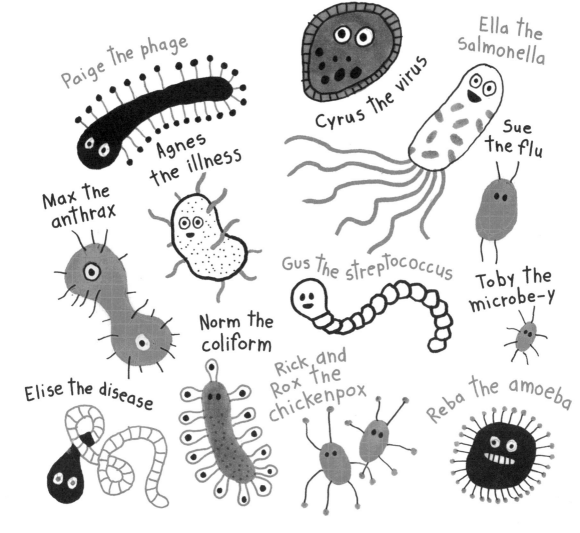

Paige the phage

Cyrus the virus

Ella the Salmonella

Agnes the illness

Sue the flu

Max the anthrax

Gus the streptococcus

Toby the microbe-y

Norm the coliform

Elise the disease

Rick and Rox the chickenpox

Reba the amoeba

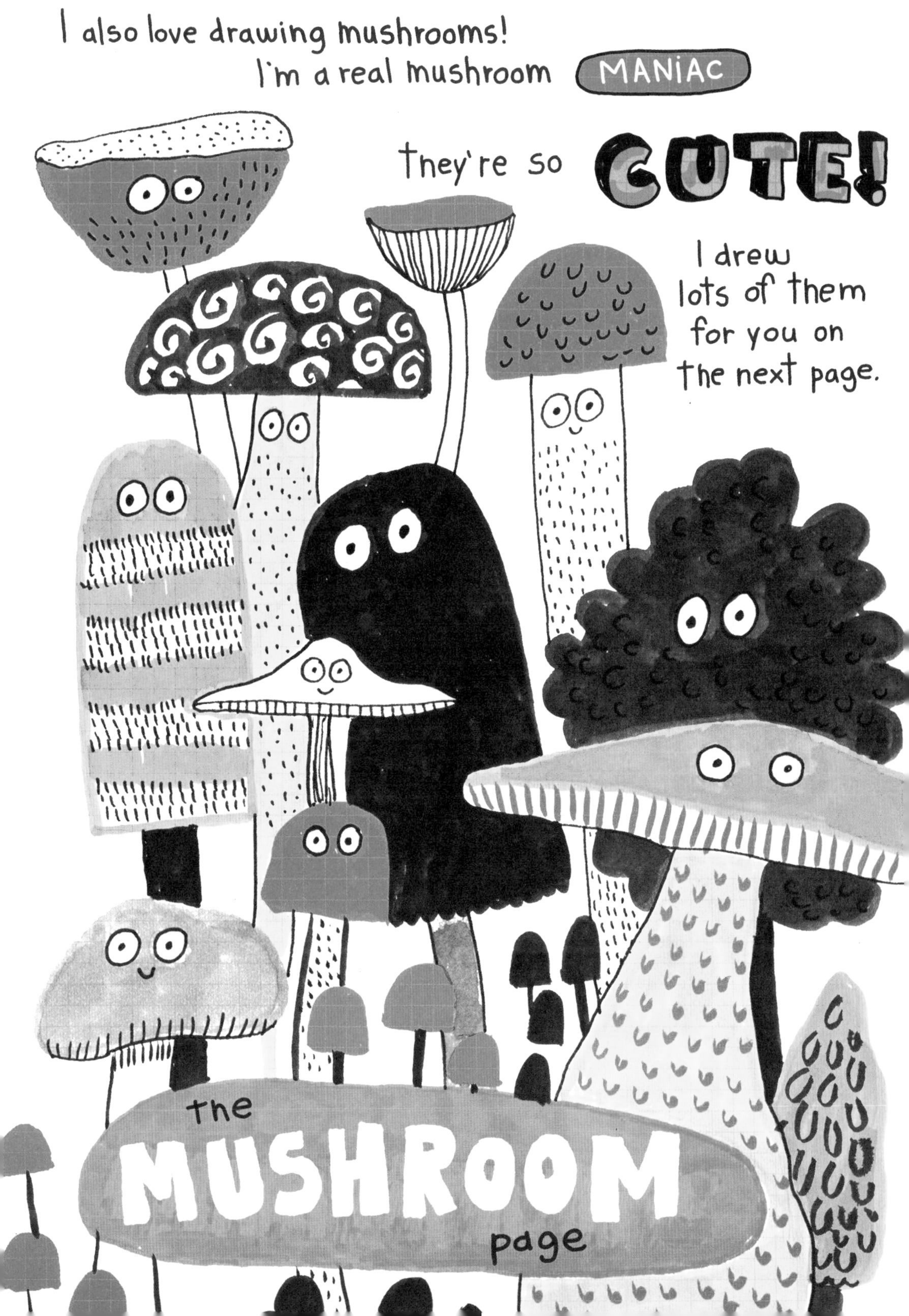
I also love drawing mushrooms!
I'm a real mushroom MANIAC
they're so CUTE!
I drew lots of them for you on the next page.
the MUSHROOM page

I LIKE **HUNTING** FOR mushrooms!

I find them strange and fascinating. Here are several that you might find while walking in the countryside.

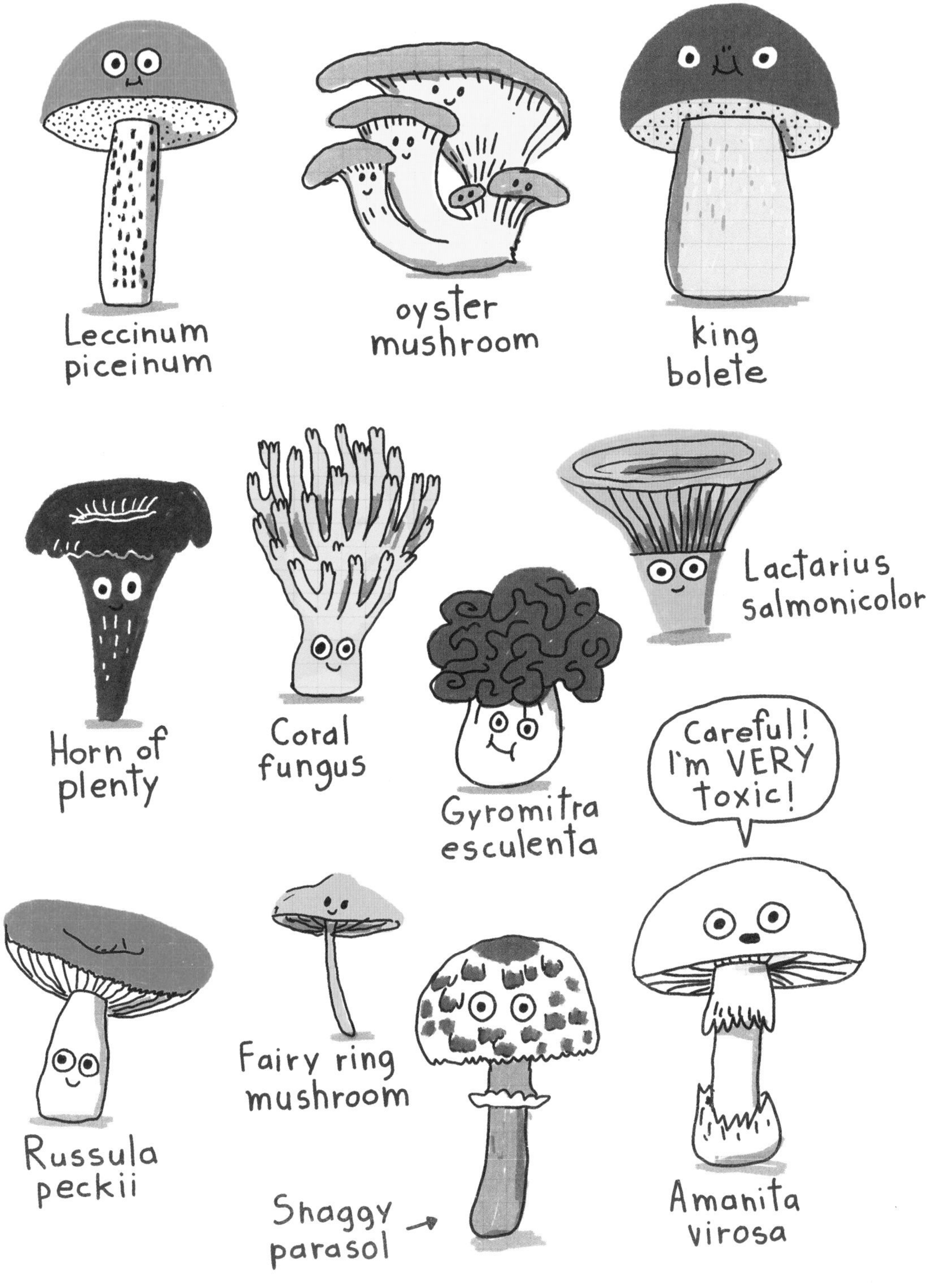
Leccinum piceinum
oyster mushroom
king bolete
Horn of plenty
Coral fungus
Gyromitra esculenta
Lactarius salmonicolor
Careful! I'm VERY toxic!
Russula peckii
Fairy ring mushroom
Shaggy parasol
Amanita virosa

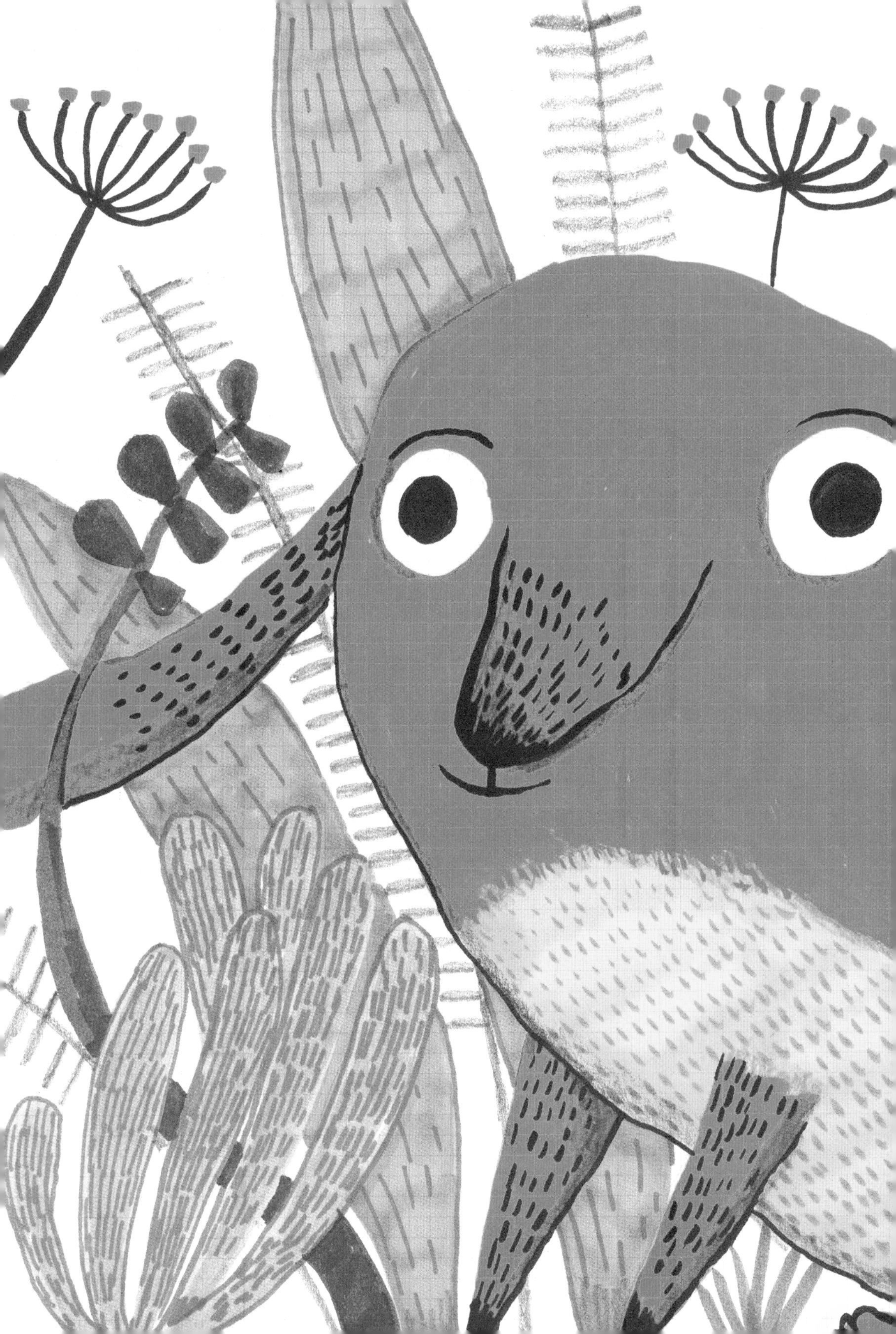

This is Bernard.
He's a mix between a rabbit, a fox, and a guinea pig. He lives off pinecones, all alone in the woods. He likes being tickled between the ears.

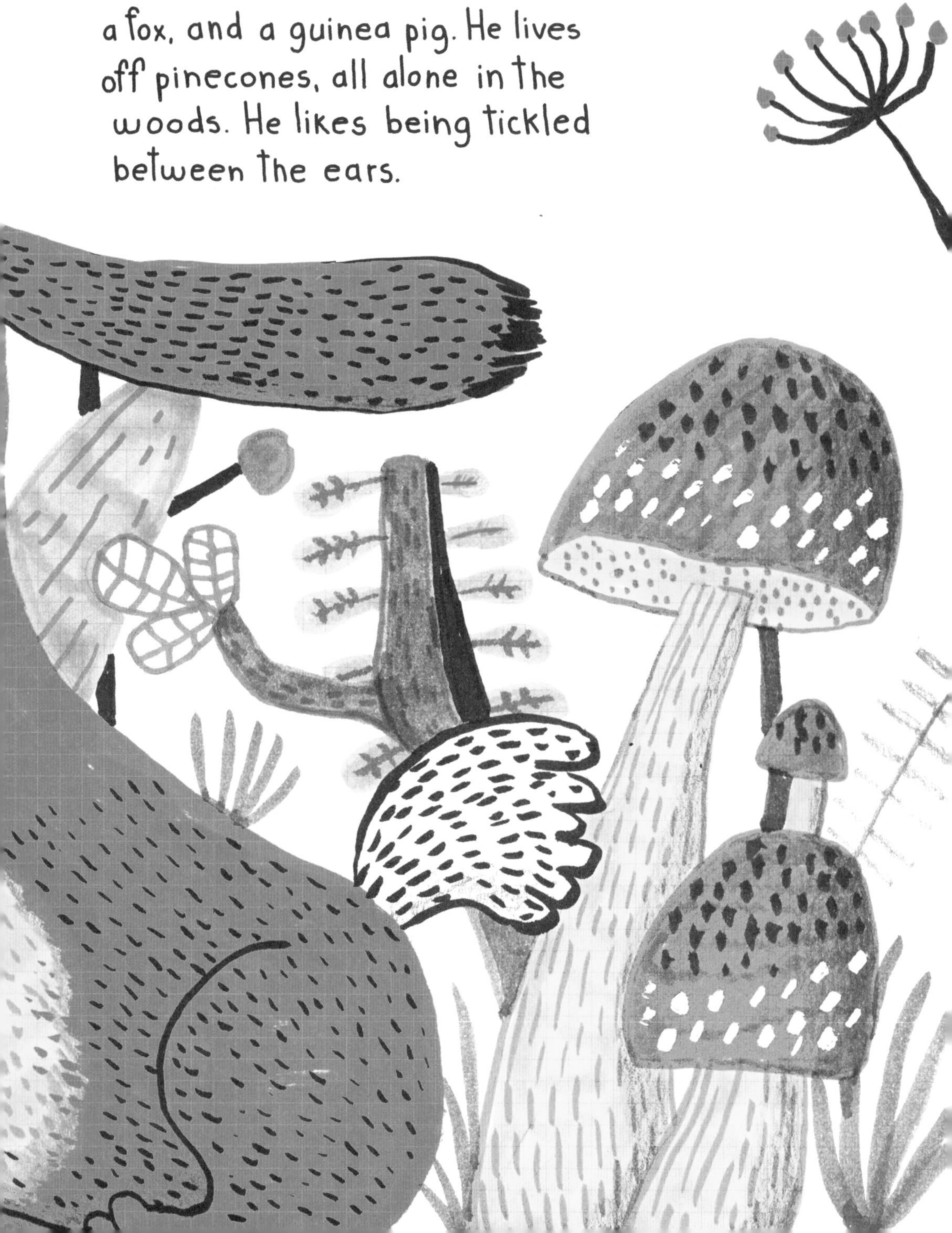

THE GLOPPLE

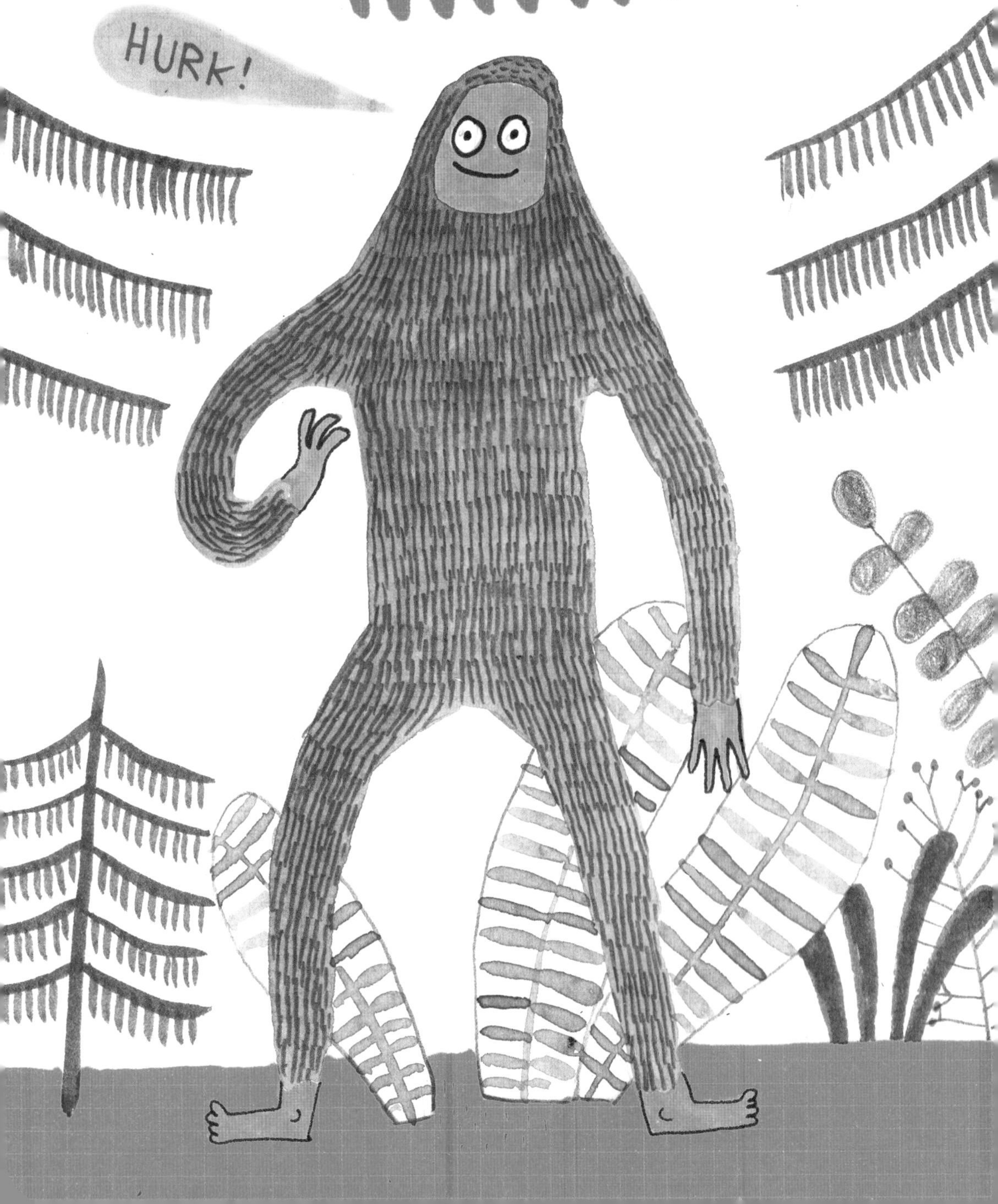
HURK!

Presenting: the glopple.
A close cousin of the Yeti and the sasquatch, he's a kind of monster that lives in Nordic forests.

He eats mostly plants, like wild pickles and arctic mangoes. He's also really good at harvesting oysters and clams. He carefully keeps the shells to give to his mother as presents.

He knows how to build a campfire and likes to roast forest marshmallows while singing weird songs that sound kind of like burps.

DRAWING HEDGEHOGS

is fun and relaxing.
Give it a try, you'll see!
(Plus, they're super cute.)

Look, since I'm incredibly kind and generous, I'll share my

ULTRA SECRET

AND

EASY PEASY

technique with you.

Vampires

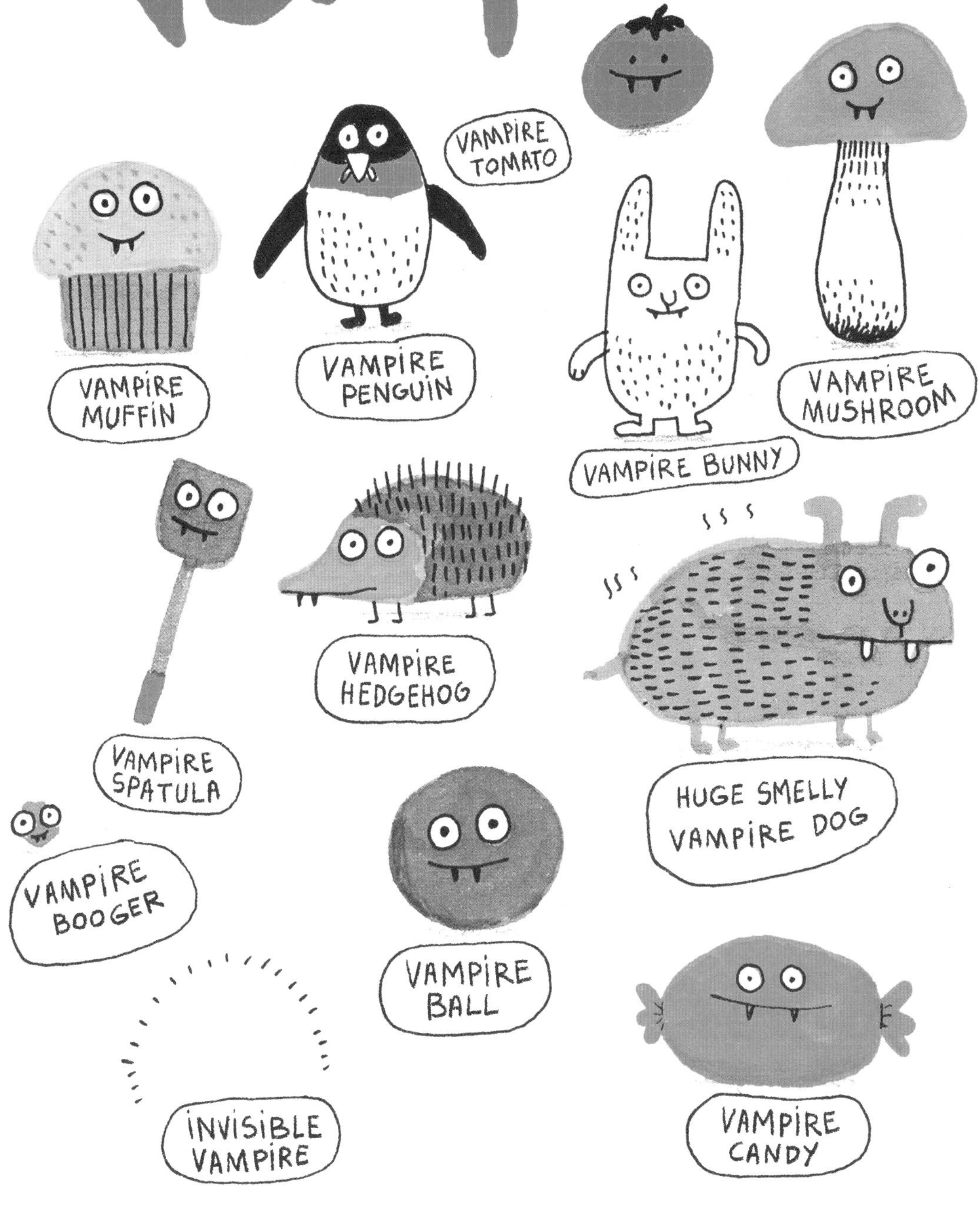
VAMPIRE TOMATO
VAMPIRE MUFFIN
VAMPIRE PENGUIN
VAMPIRE BUNNY
VAMPIRE MUSHROOM
VAMPIRE SPATULA
VAMPIRE HEDGEHOG
HUGE SMELLY VAMPIRE DOG
VAMPIRE BOOGER
VAMPIRE BALL
INVISIBLE VAMPIRE
VAMPIRE CANDY

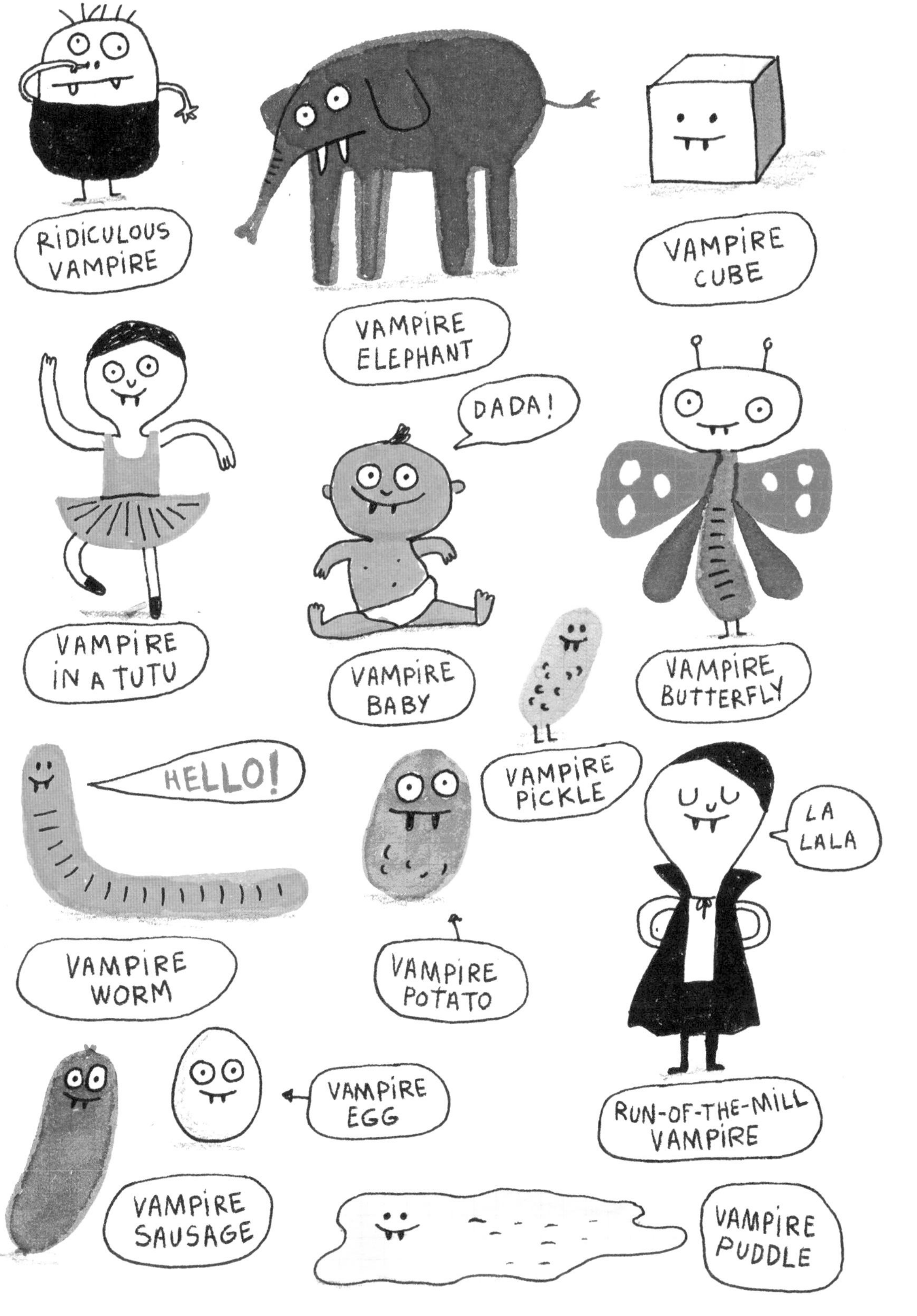
RIDICULOUS VAMPIRE
VAMPIRE ELEPHANT
VAMPIRE CUBE
VAMPIRE IN A TUTU
DADA!
VAMPIRE BABY
VAMPIRE BUTTERFLY
VAMPIRE PICKLE
HELLO!
VAMPIRE WORM
VAMPIRE POTATO
LA LALA
RUN-OF-THE-MILL VAMPIRE
VAMPIRE EGG
VAMPIRE SAUSAGE
VAMPIRE PUDDLE

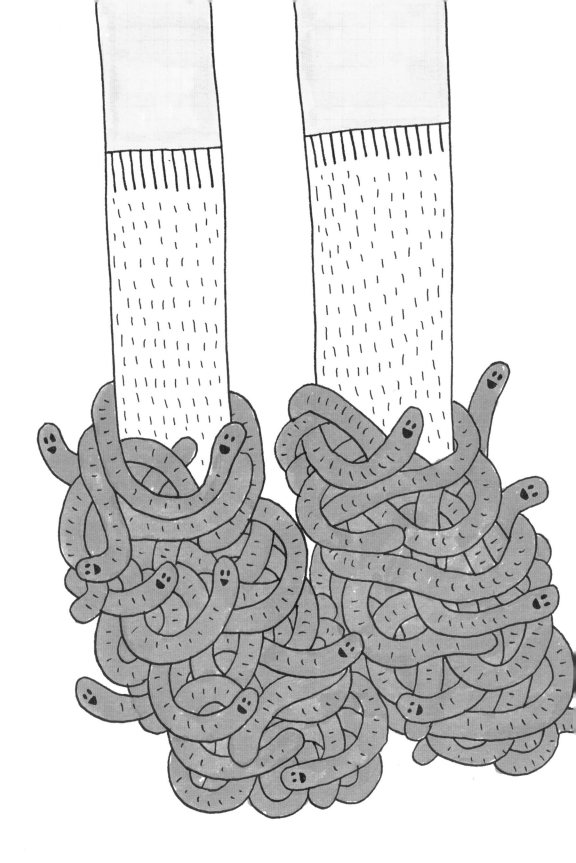

FABULOUS

WORM SLIPPERS

for sale!

comfortable! slimy!

original!

No one else will have slippers

LIKE THESE

THE REAL BLACK NOTEBOOK

On my
REAL
desk

with
REAL
clutter

and a
REAL
cookie.

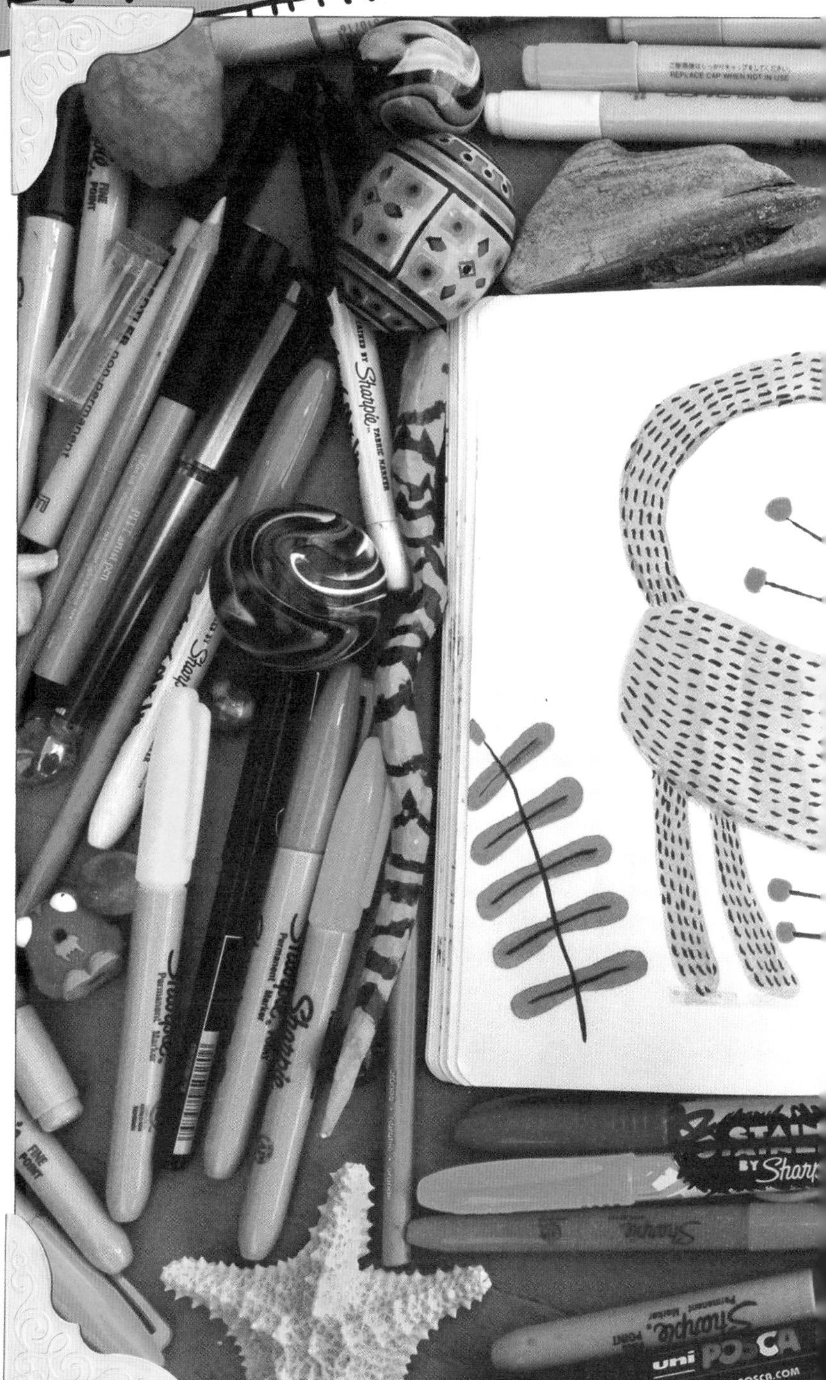

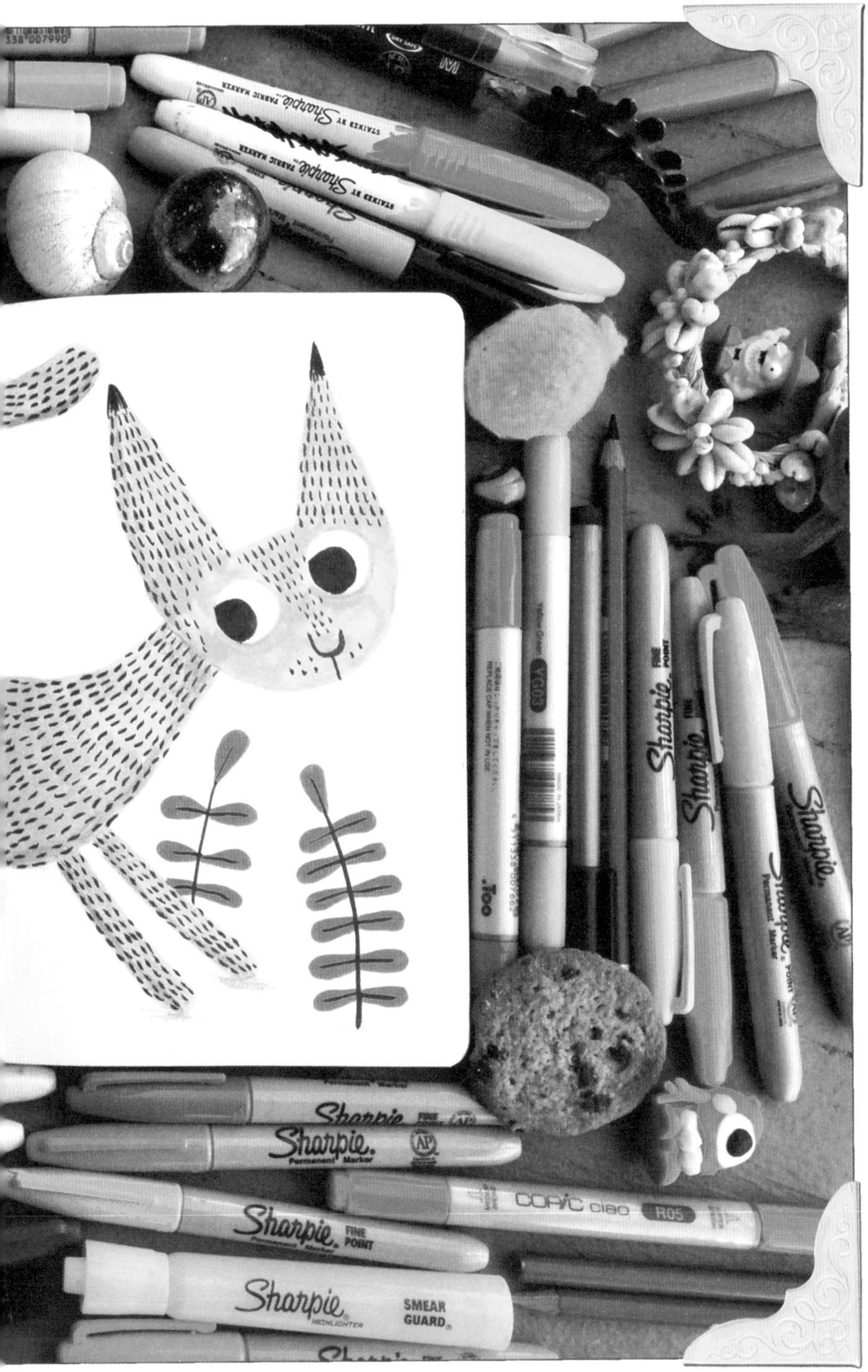

Sharpie.
FINE POINT
Permanent Marker
COPIC ciao
R05
Sharpie.
HIGHLIGHTER
SMEAR GUARD

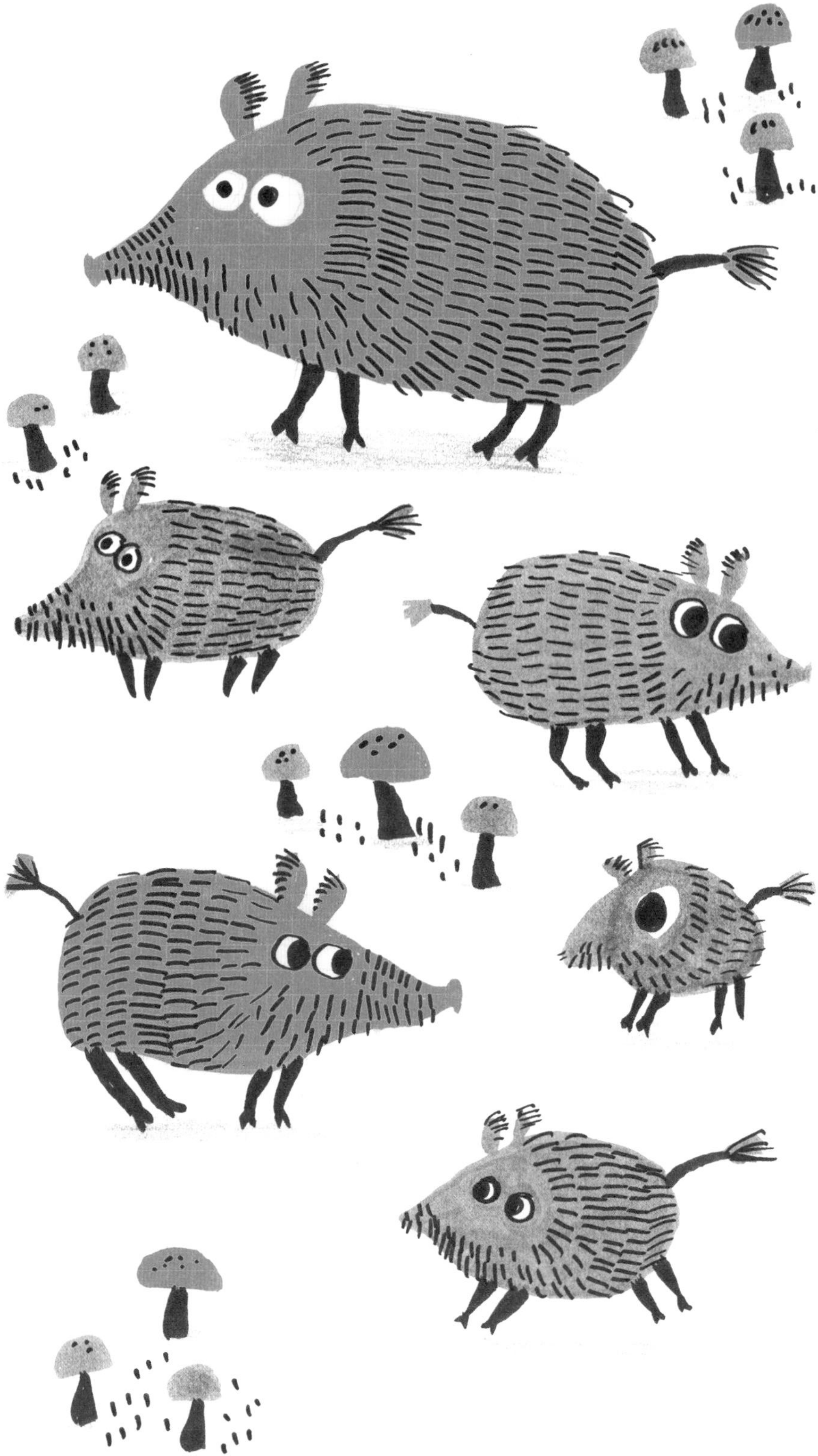

So you want to be an illustrator?
Here's my

ADVICE

1 Draw all the time! Draw anything and everything! Try to imitate the illustrations from your favourite books. It's okay to copy them—it's a great way to learn. You can even trace them. This helps you to understand how to draw curves and lines.

2 Don't be afraid about making mistakes! This is my most important piece of advice. I make mistakes all the time. If you think your drawing is ugly, just take a deep breath and start again.

3 Don't get discouraged. Even the most successful artists are dissatisfied with their work sometimes.

4 There's no magic to this work. The secret is practice. Lots of practice. Enormous amounts of practice. That's how you improve.

ANATOLE

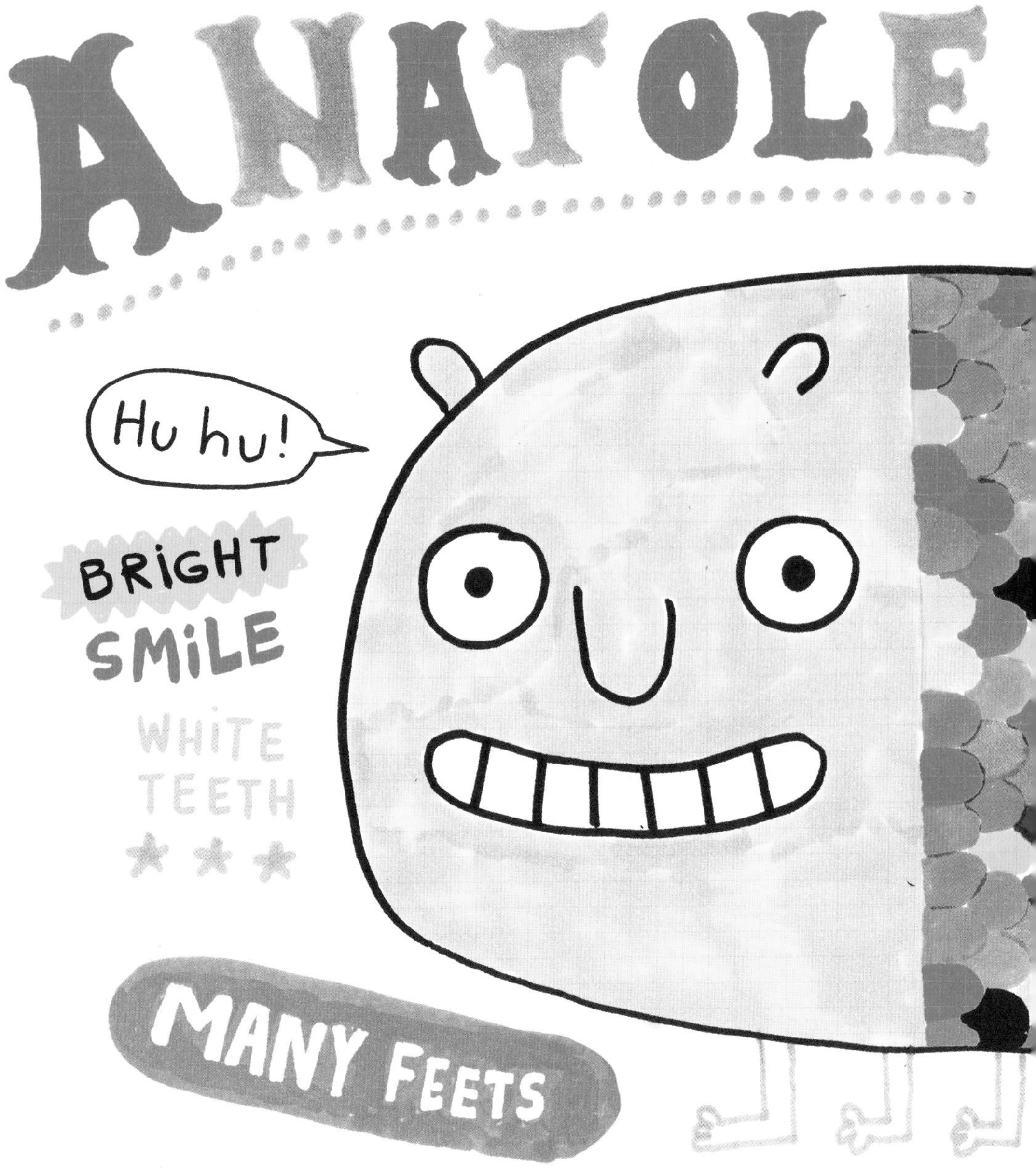
Hu hu!
BRIGHT
SMILE
WHITE
TEETH
MANY FEETS

Like I said in the title, Anatole is the crazy creature who lives in Nicole's school. He sleeps in the principal's desk drawer.

THE CRAZY CREATURE

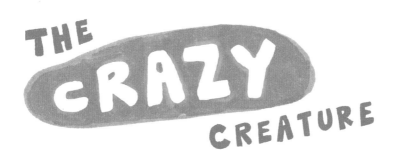

WHO LIVES IN NICOLE'S SCHOOL

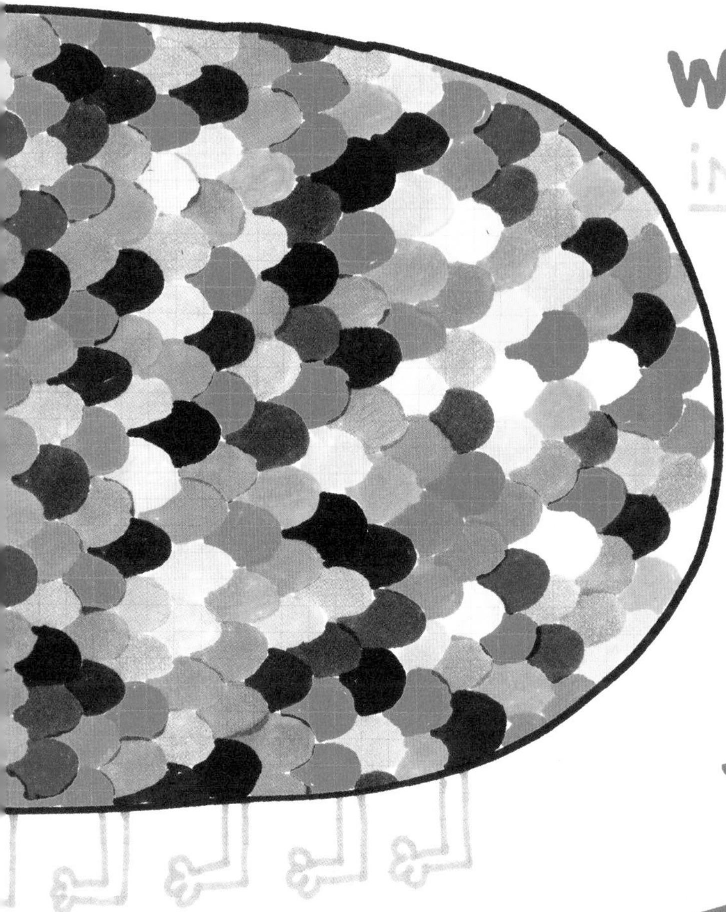

This is NICOLE

↓

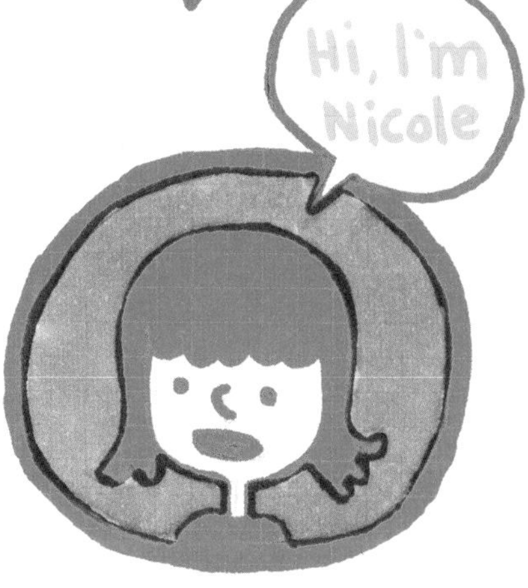
Hi, I'm Nicole

Normally, he just laughs and dances all day, but sometimes he steals erasers from the kids so he can snack on them.

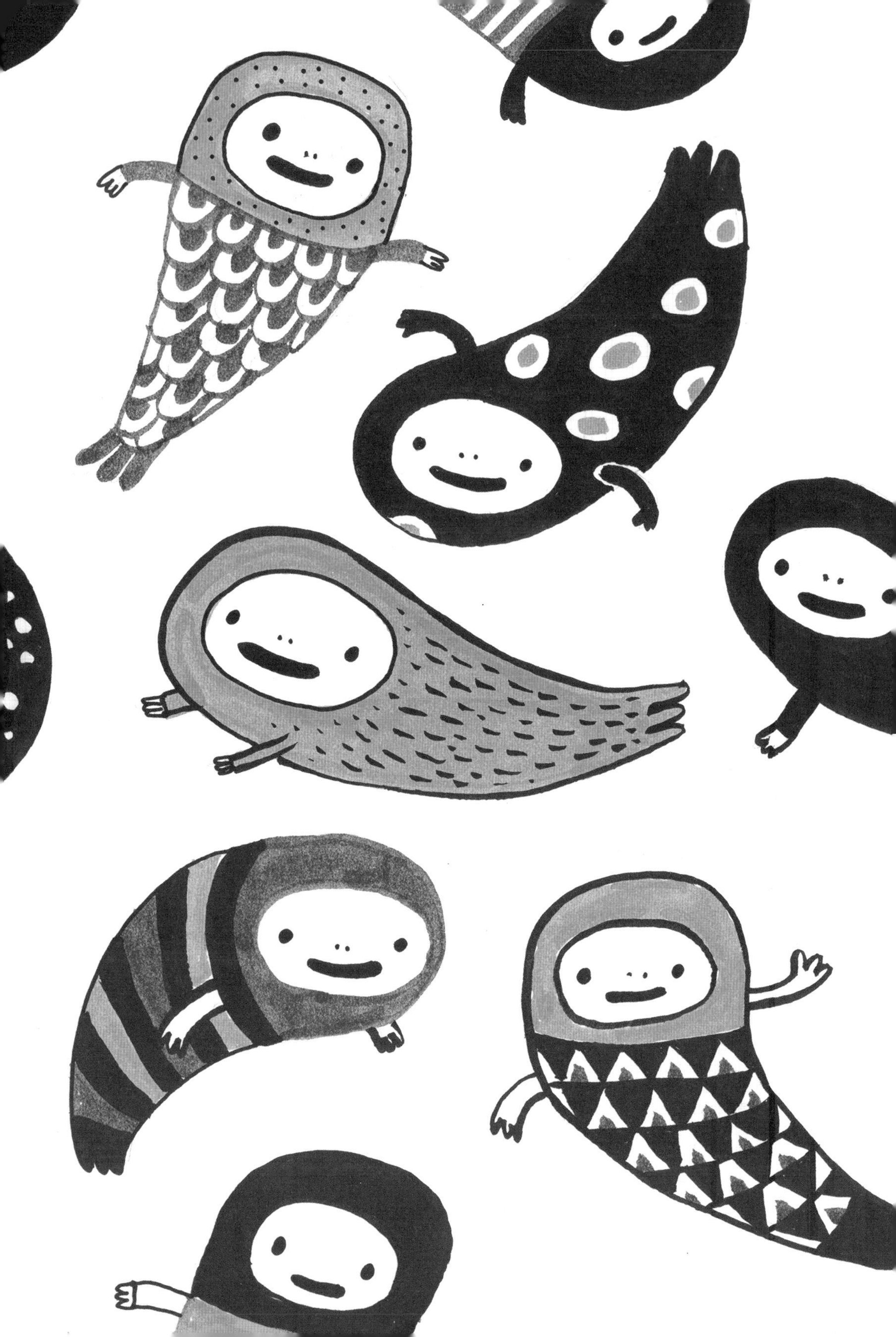

THE FLIBBERTY-WHIPPETS
FROM THE NORTHERN SEAS

The flibberty-whippets are part of the will-o-the-wisps aquatic family. They swim in cold-water seas and live off plankton and foam bubbles.

If you are very, very lucky, you can see them in the early mornings when the aurora borealis appear; they love the aurora borealis and will sometimes jump out of the water to see them.

The flibberty-whippets are amphibious creatures—they can live in water or on land. They fly very quickly and are scared stiff of humans.

THIS IS ANASTASIA.

HAIRDRESSER AND STYLIST TO RENOWNED MONSTERS **WORLDWIDE.**

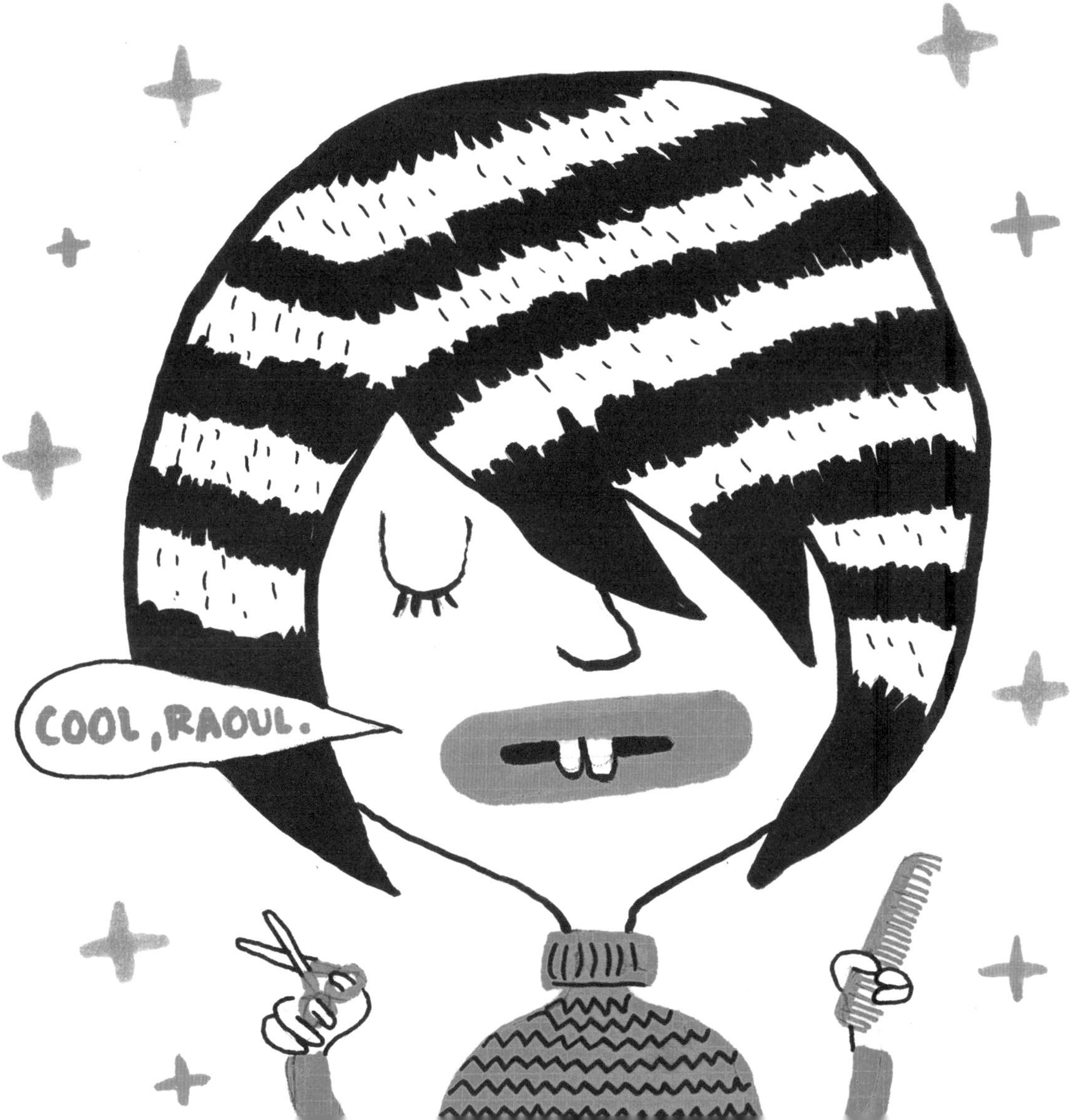
COOL, RAOUL.

And here are a few of her vibrant and breathtaking

CREATIONS:

style: "zero gravity"
model: Fulpin Znif

style: "Feather duster from space"
model: Rogrop Xolp

style: "Red current Jelly"
model: Trsflpk Mott

style: "Pink Emo"
model: Glip Glip

ROCK ON.

style: "Little Prankster"
model: Turlup Xu

ON THE PLANET

FLON,

THERE ARE:

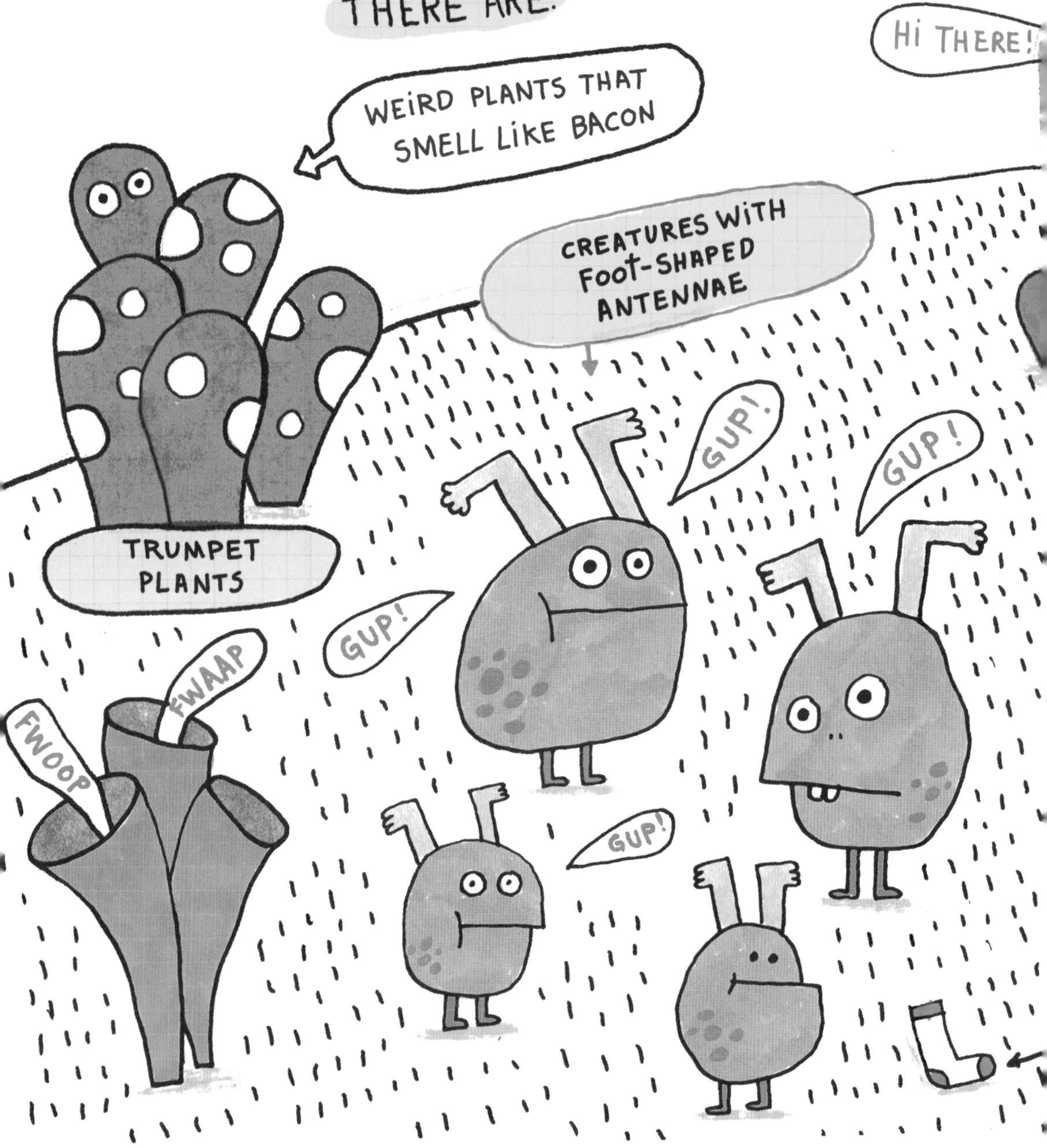

Hi THERE!
WEiRD PLANTS THAT SMELL LiKE BACON
CREATURES WiTH Foot-SHAPED ANTENNAE
TRUMPET PLANTS
GUP!
GUP!
GUP!
GUP!
FWAAP
FWOOP

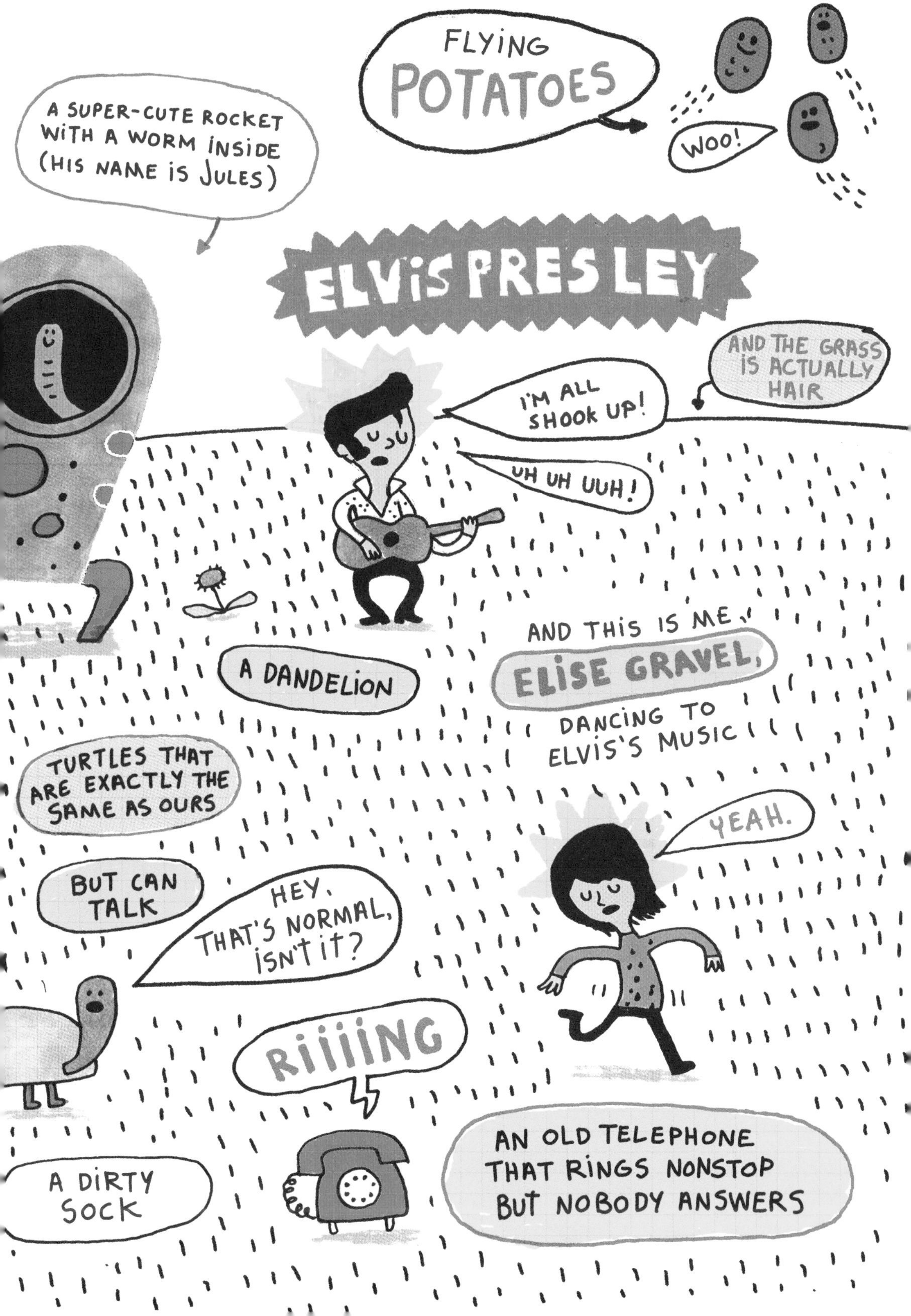
FLYING POTATOES
WOO!
A SUPER-CUTE ROCKET WITH A WORM INSIDE (HIS NAME IS JULES)
ELVIS PRESLEY
AND THE GRASS IS ACTUALLY HAIR
I'M ALL SHOOK UP!
UH UH UUH!
A DANDELION
AND THIS IS ME,
ELISE GRAVEL,
DANCING TO ELVIS'S MUSIC
TURTLES THAT ARE EXACTLY THE SAME AS OURS
BUT CAN TALK
HEY, THAT'S NORMAL, ISN'T IT?
YEAH.
RIIIING
A DIRTY SOCK
AN OLD TELEPHONE THAT RINGS NONSTOP BUT NOBODY ANSWERS

I have to tell you something,
but don't tell my husband
because he'll be jealous.
It's a secret between you
and me, okay?

Here it is:
I'm a little in love with E.t.

I think he's

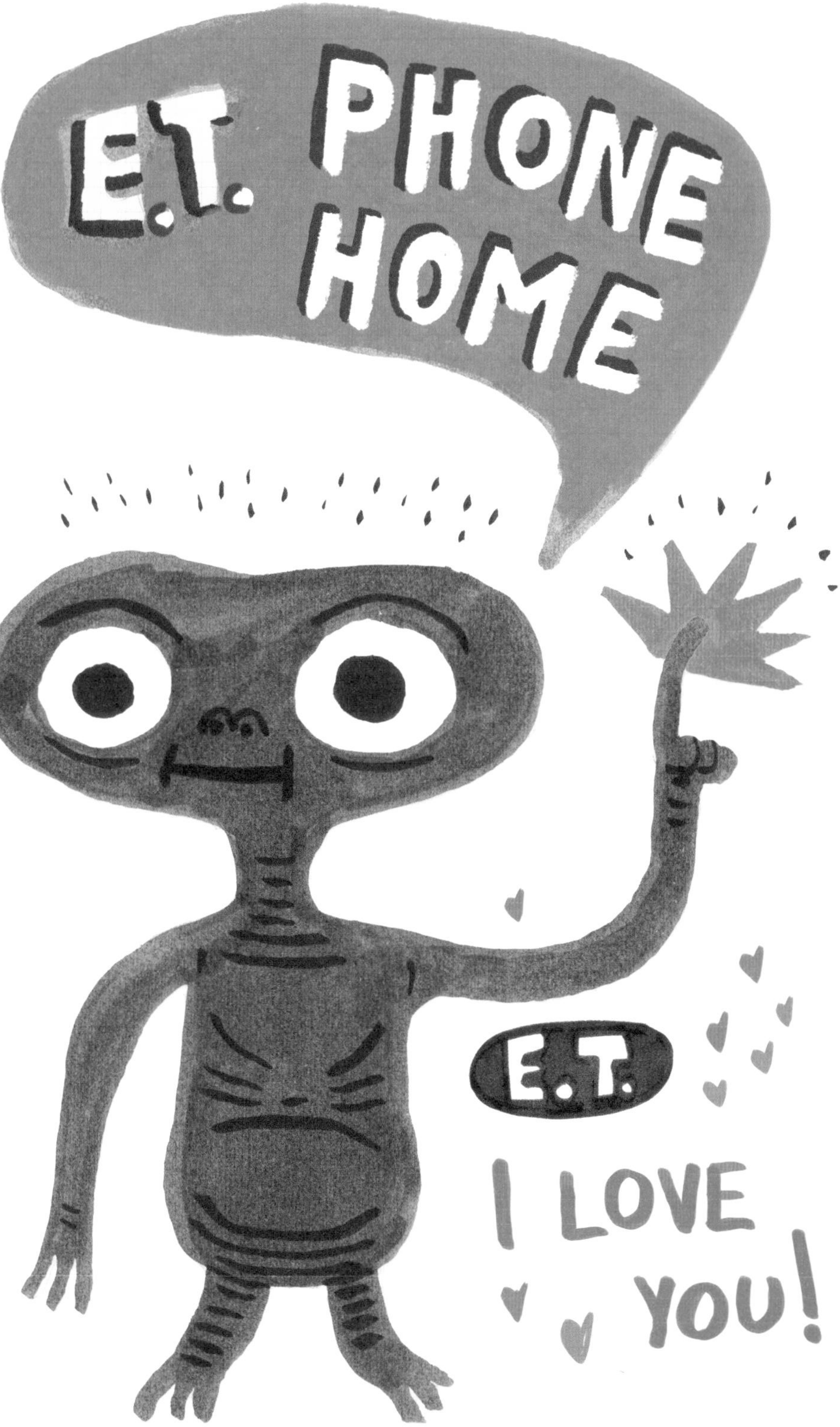
E.T. PHONE HOME
E.T.
I LOVE YOU!

THIS is

MARVIN,

the man with
lots of stuff
in his

BEARD

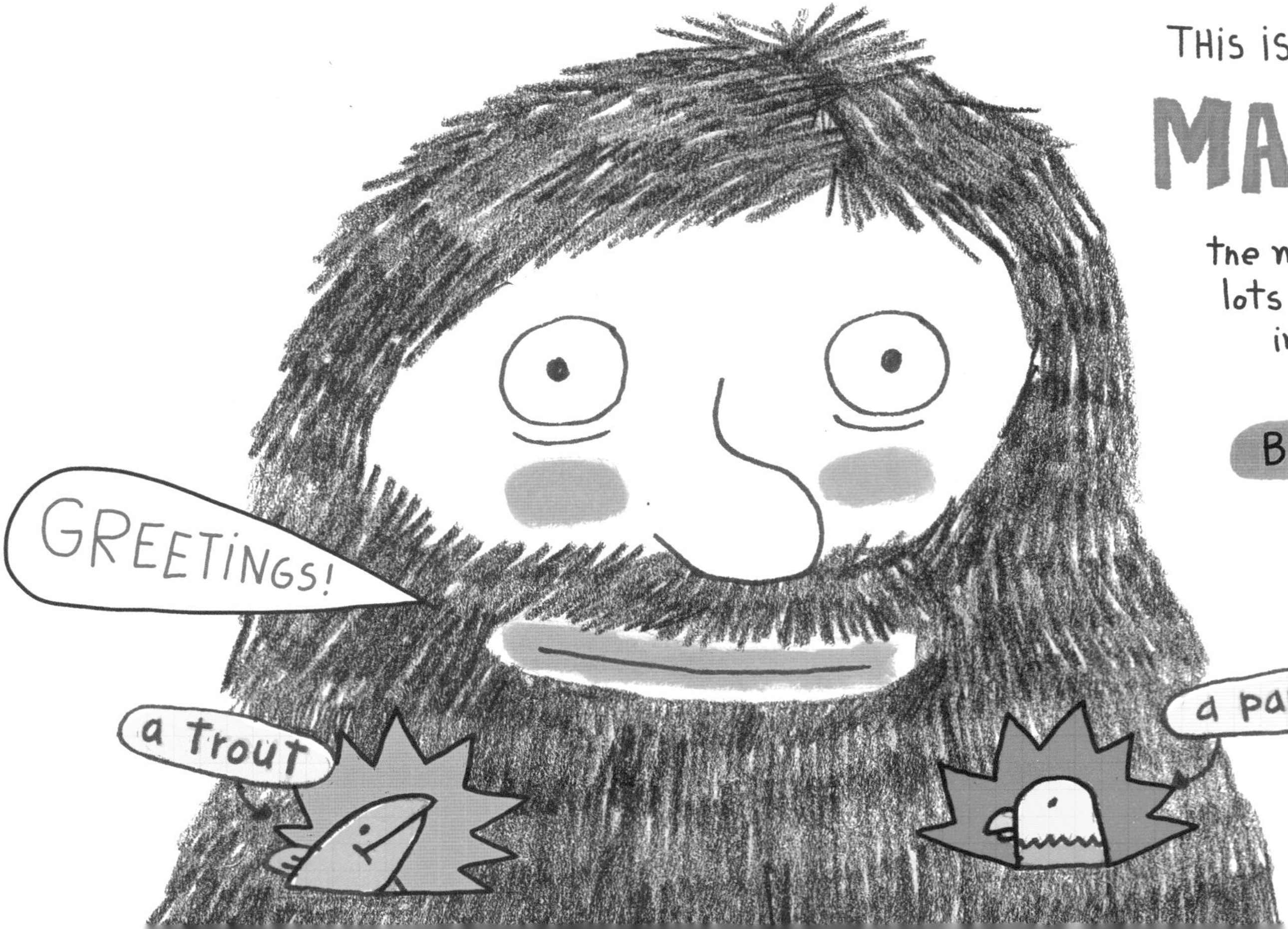
GREETINGS!
a trout
a parakeet

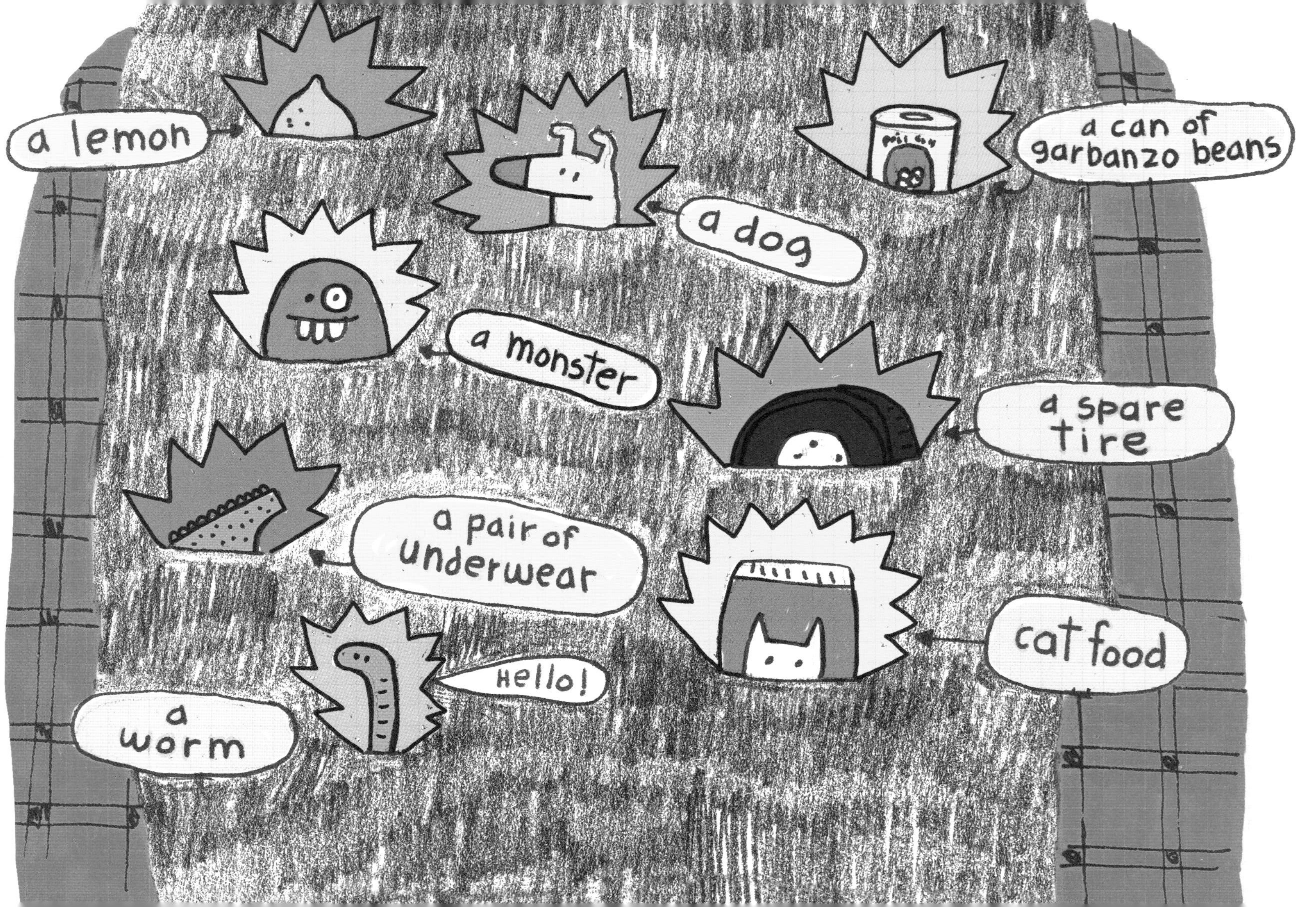
a lemon
a dog
a can of garbanzo beans
a monster
a spare tire
a pair of underwear
cat food
Hello!
a worm

A PAGE OF

SMALL CREATURES

You know me, right? I'm a huge fan of little critters.

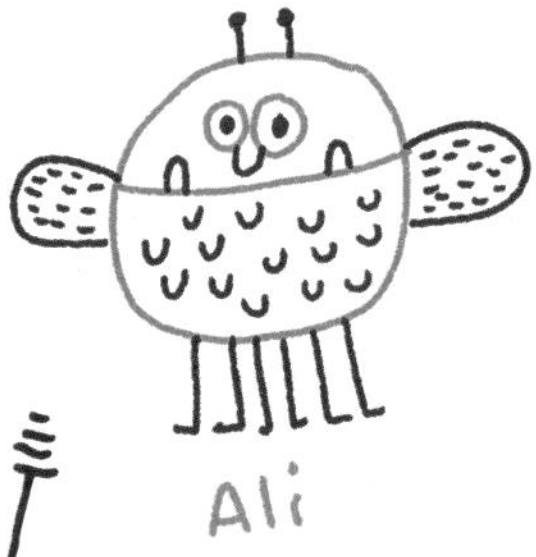
Ali

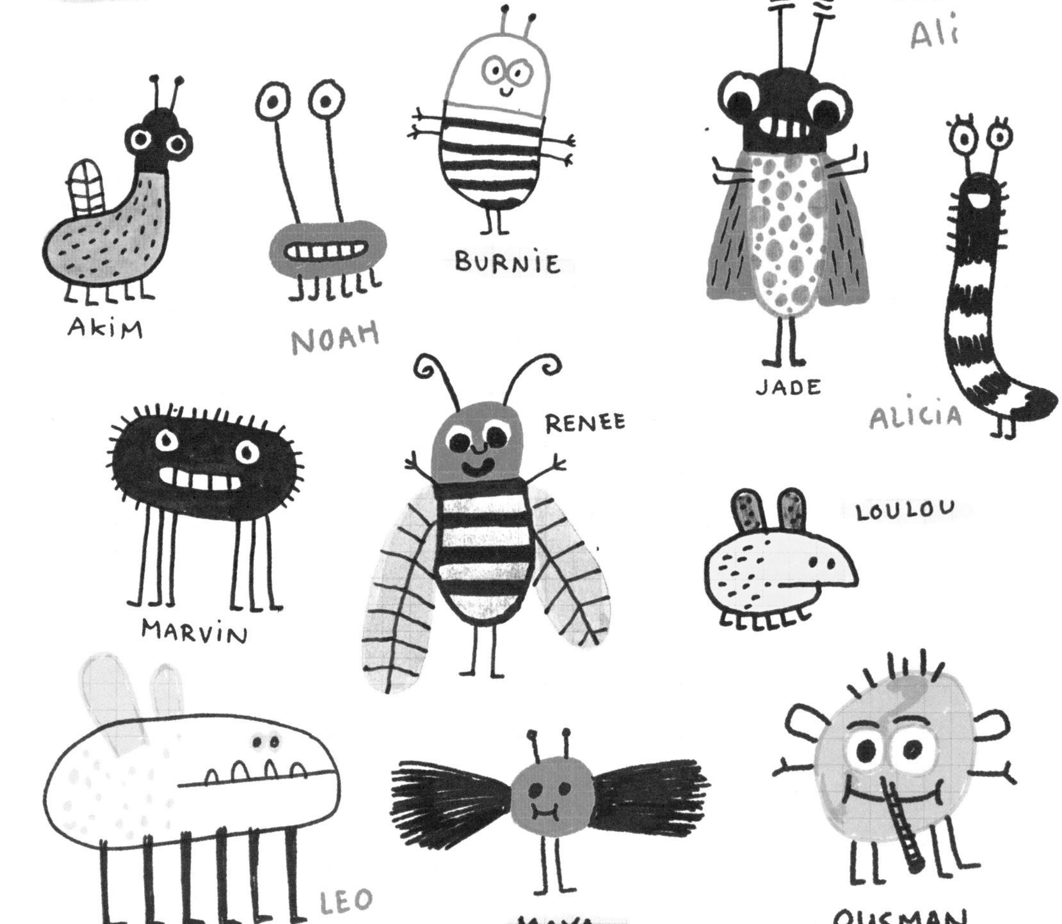
AKIM
NOAH
BURNIE
JADE
ALICIA
RENEE
MARVIN
LOULOU
LEO
MAYA
OUSMAN

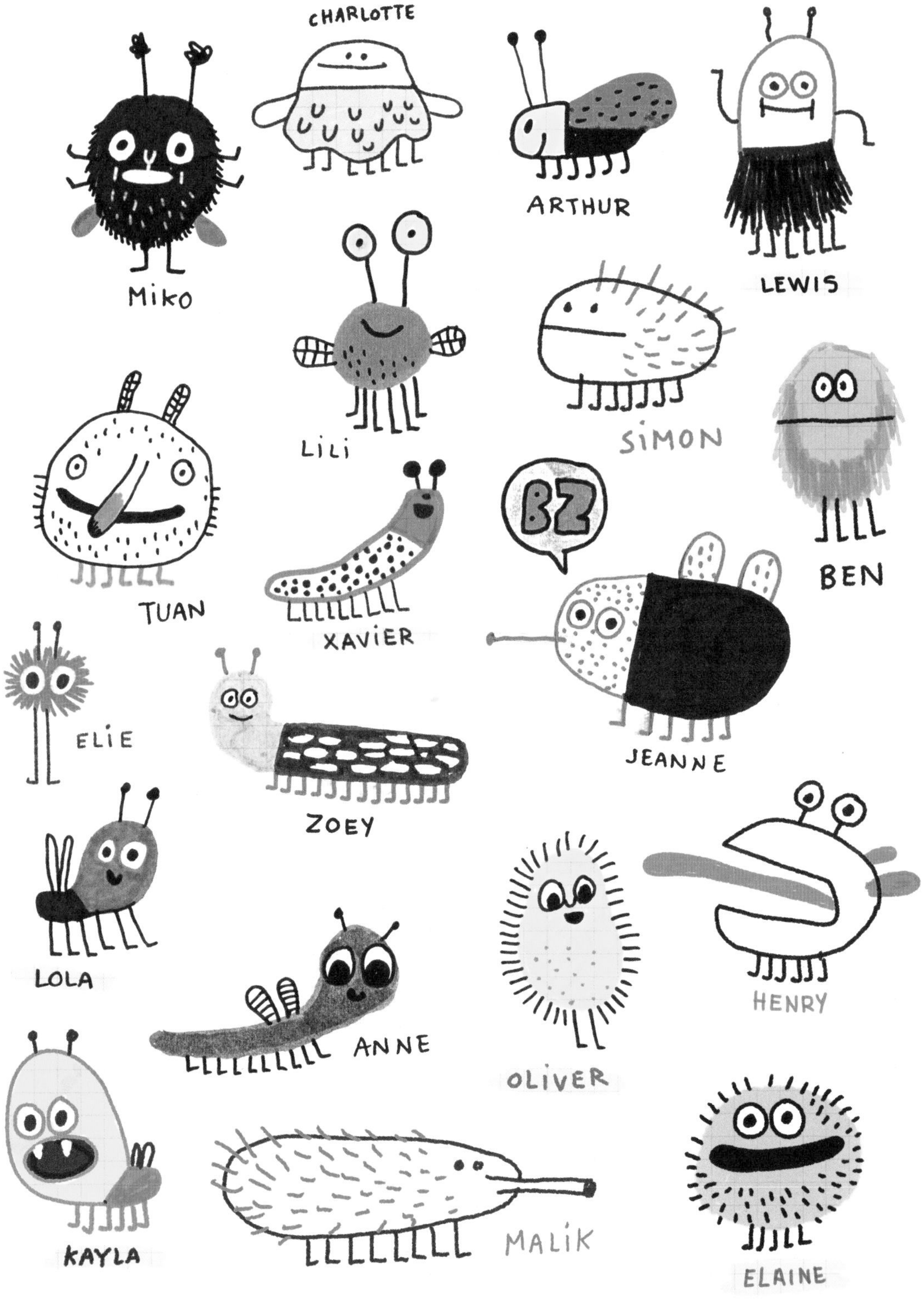
CHARLOTTE
ARTHUR
MIKO
LEWIS
LILI
SIMON
BEN
TUAN
BZ
XAVIER
ELIE
JEANNE
ZOEY
LOLA
HENRY
ANNE
OLIVER
KAYLA
MALIK
ELAINE

The true story of the little

CROW GIRL

This is a story I read about online.
Gabby, eight years old, liked to feed
crumbs from her lunch box to the
crows on her way home from school.
Every day. The crows got used to
Gabby and started to thank her by
bringing her little presents that
they'd found on the ground: a button,
a pearl, a Lego brick, a lost earring,
a shiny nail. And even a little
plastic heart!

Gabby collected the crows' gifts and
organized them in a little box. She had
dozens of them! She put each gift into
a little bag, on which she wrote the date
that she received it.

I'm a little bit jealous. I think I'll
start feeding crows too.

KIWIS

(A kind of bird that lives in New Zealand)

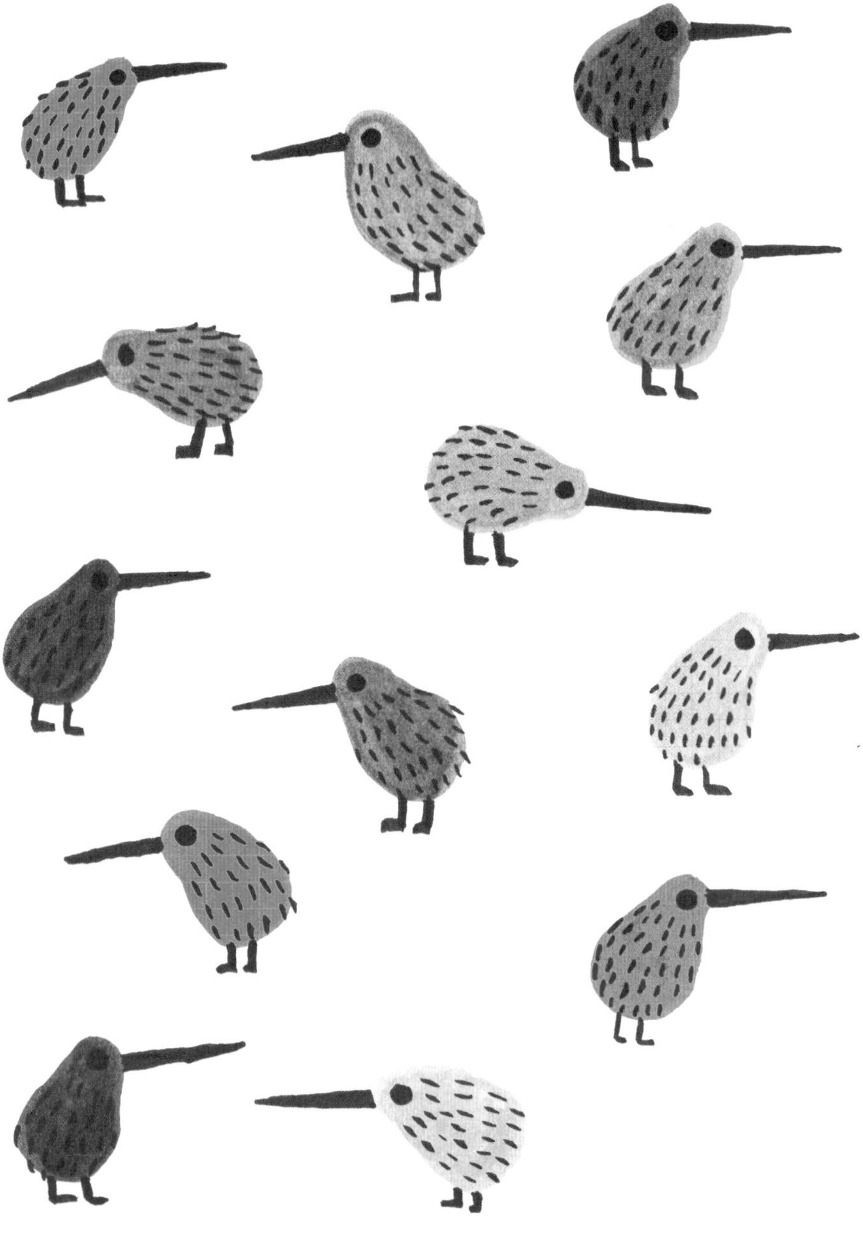

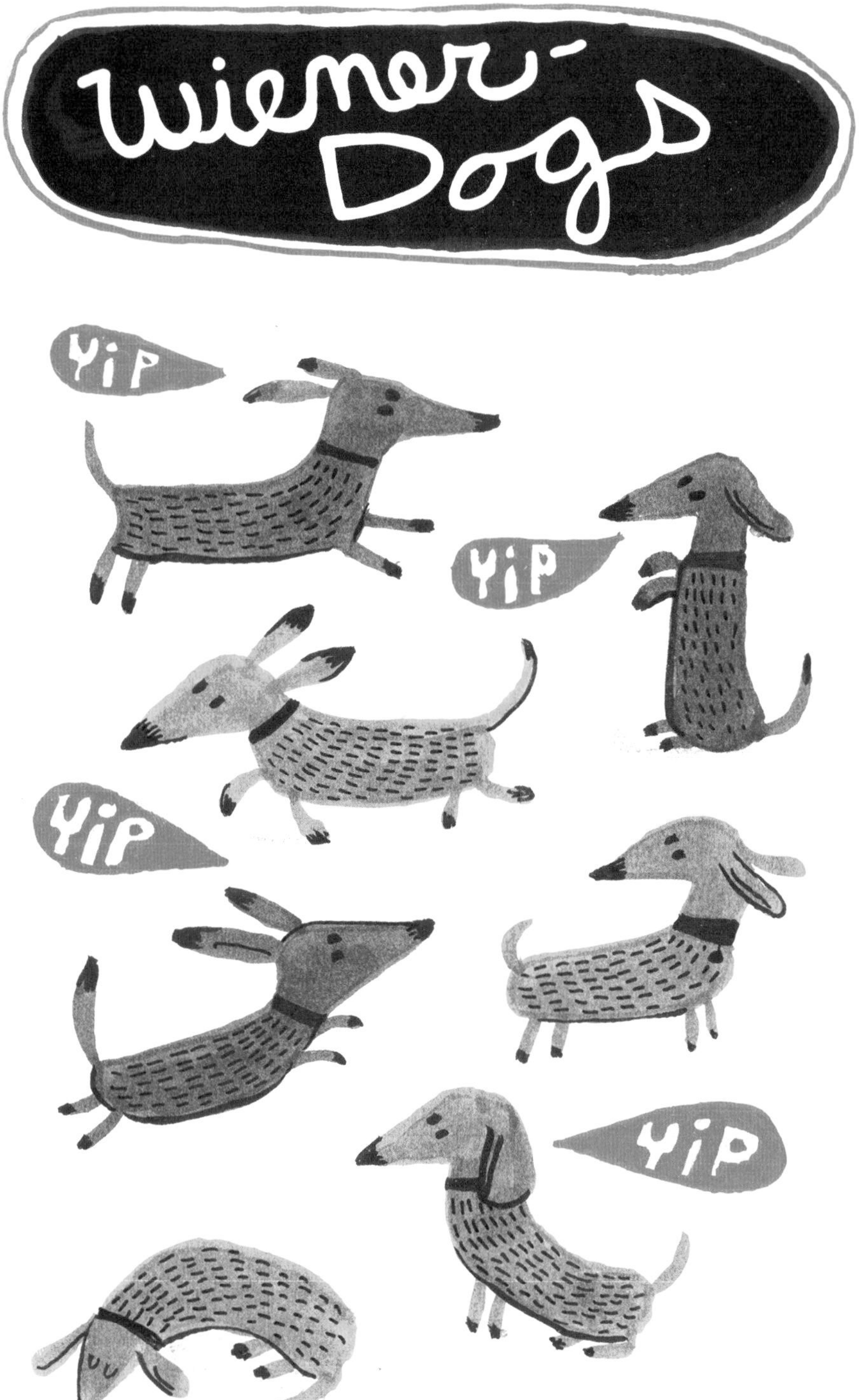
Wiener-Dogs
YIP
YIP
YIP
YIP

Okay, don't say I didn't warn you...
Here's some real nonsense:

BUNNIES

dressed in

PUNK,

ROCK

and heavy

METAL!

T-shirts!

Hey, I can do what I want!
It's MY little black notebook.

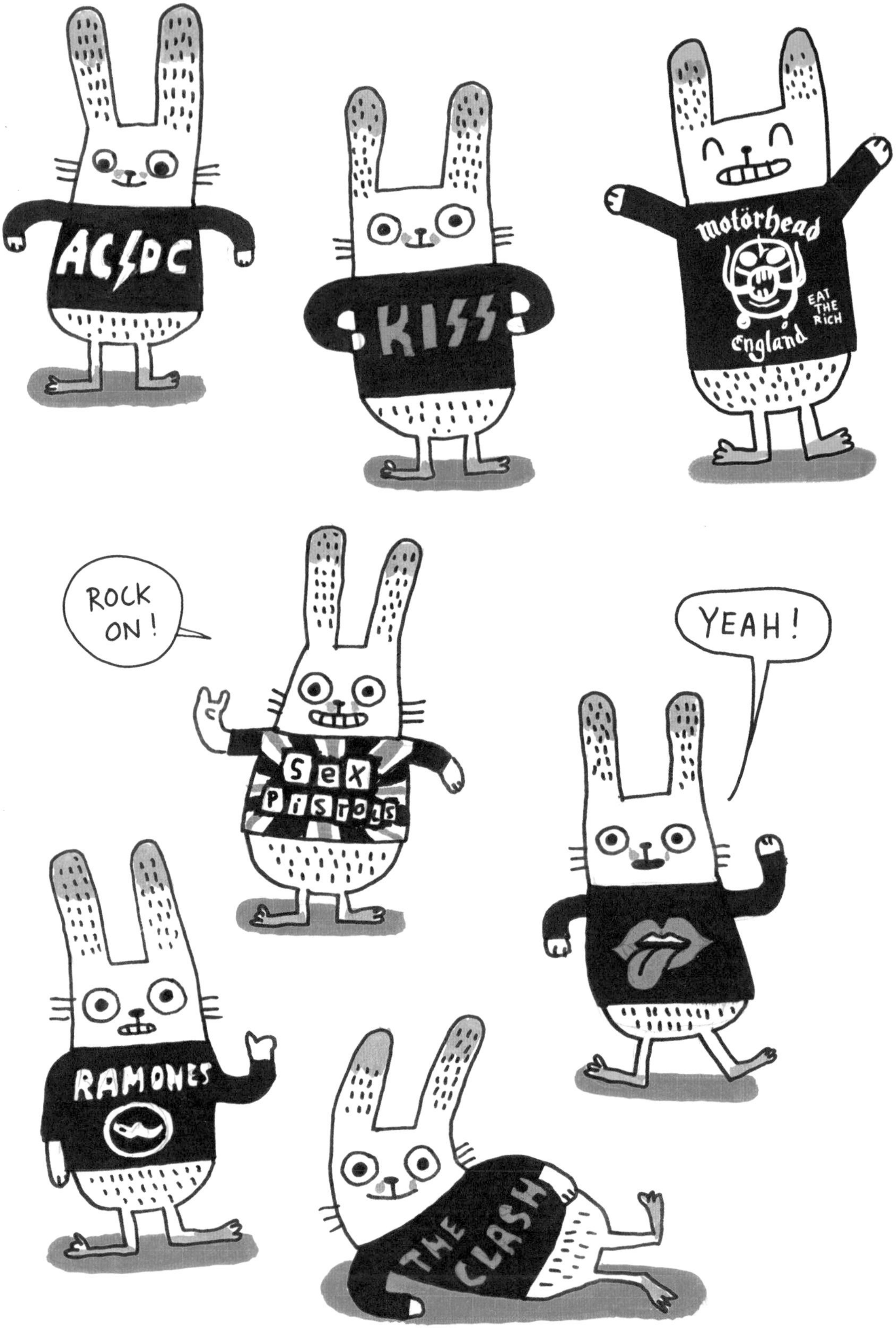
AC/DC
KISS
motörhead
England
EAT THE RICH
ROCK ON!
Sex Pistols
YEAH!
RAMONES
THE CLASH

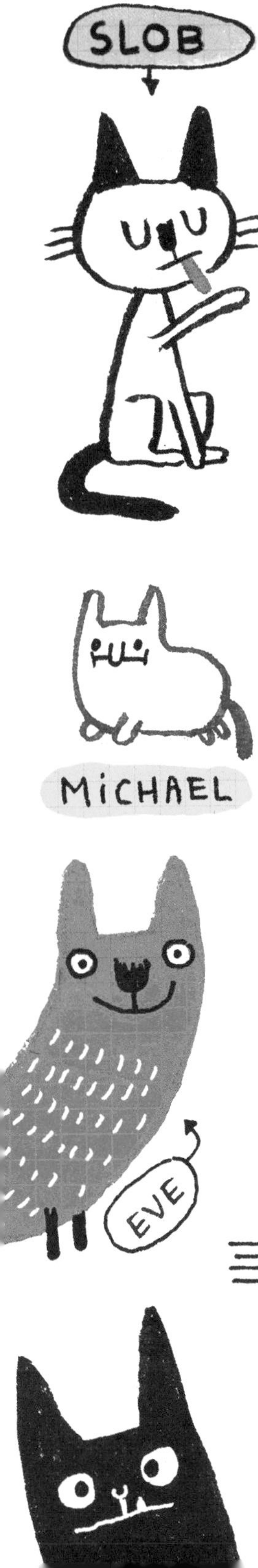
SLOB
MiCHAEL
EVE

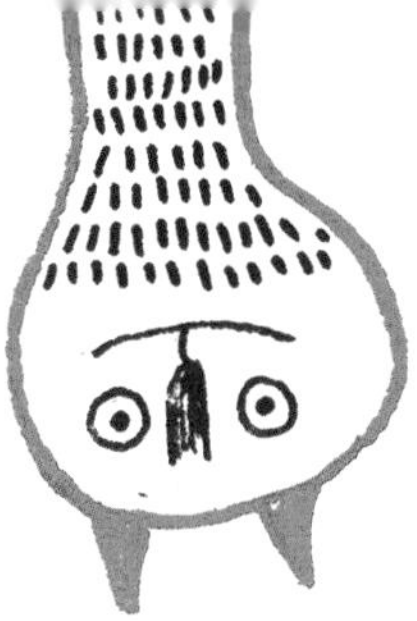

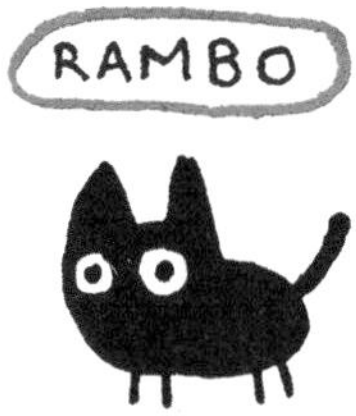
RAMBO

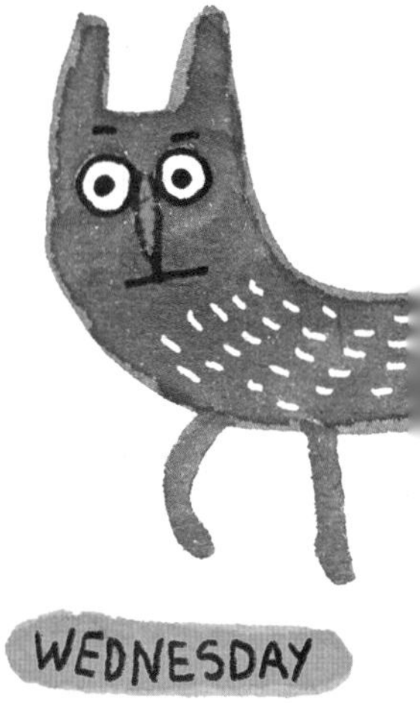
WEDNESDAY

This page is all about cats. Take off your shoes, and don't make any sudden moves. I'll let you choose your favourite.

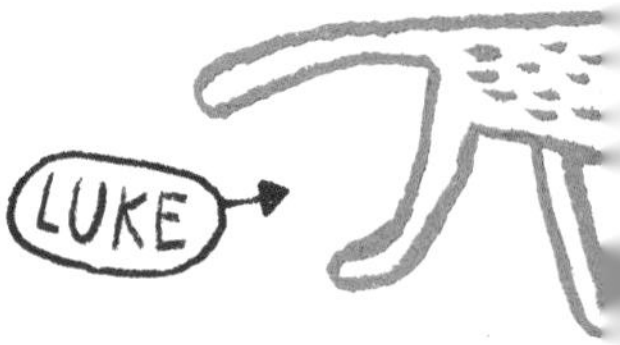
LUKE

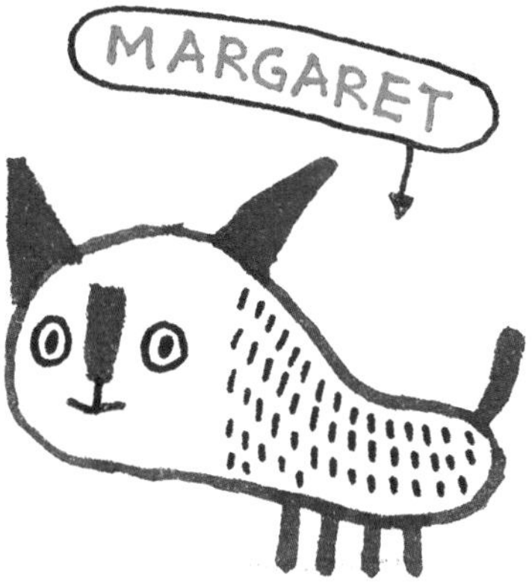
MARGARET

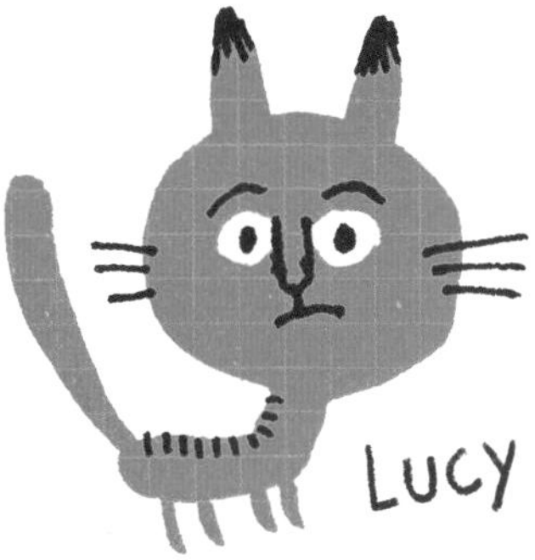
LUCY

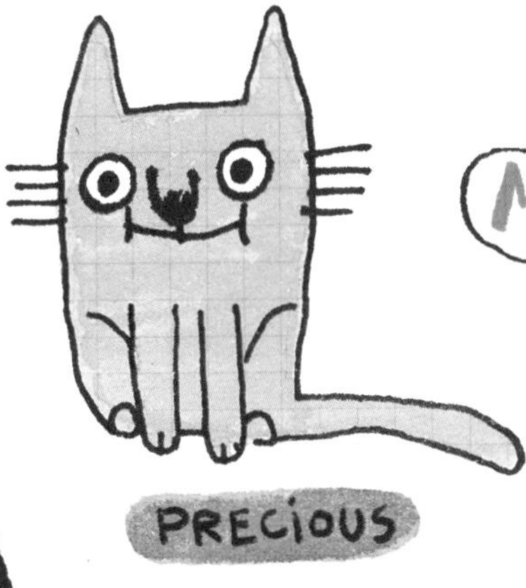
PRECiOUS

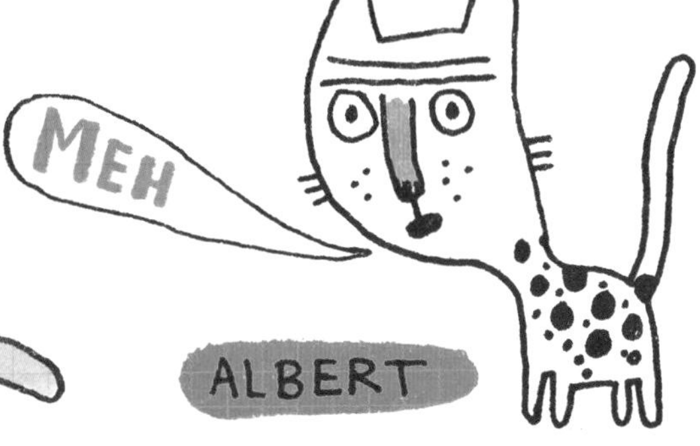
MEH
ALBERT

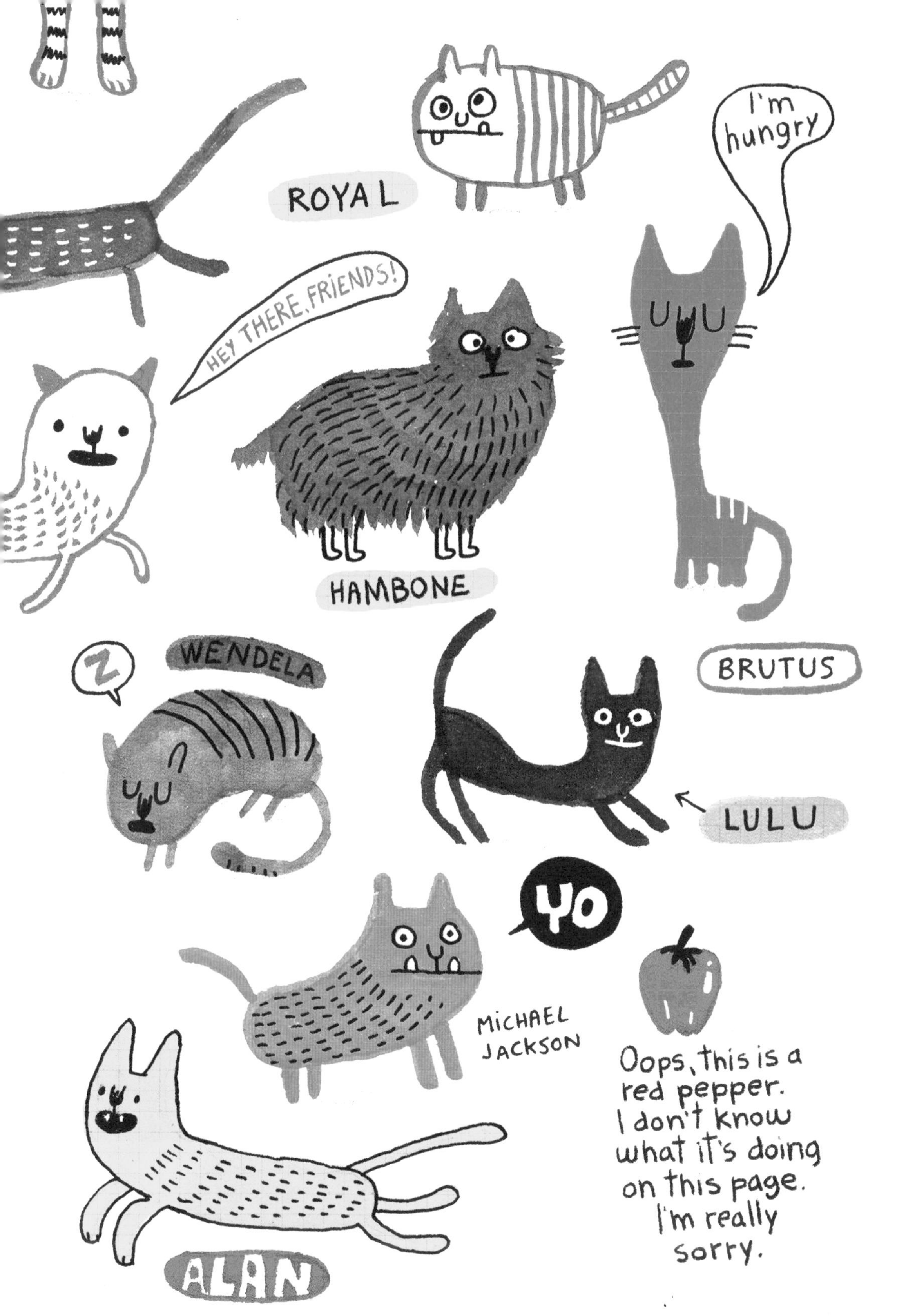

ROYAL
I'm hungry
HEY THERE, FRIENDS!
HAMBONE
BRUTUS
Z
WENDELA
LULU
YO
MICHAEL JACKSON
ALAN
Oops, this is a red pepper. I don't know what it's doing on this page. I'm really sorry.

DOGS

I love cats but I really like dogs too, especially dogs that stink and are a bit silly.

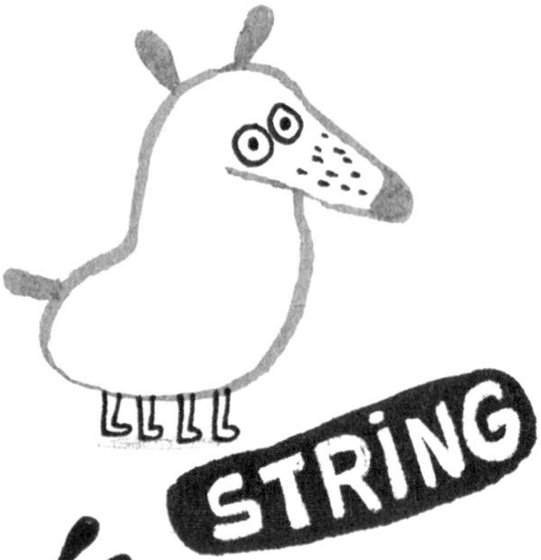

STRING

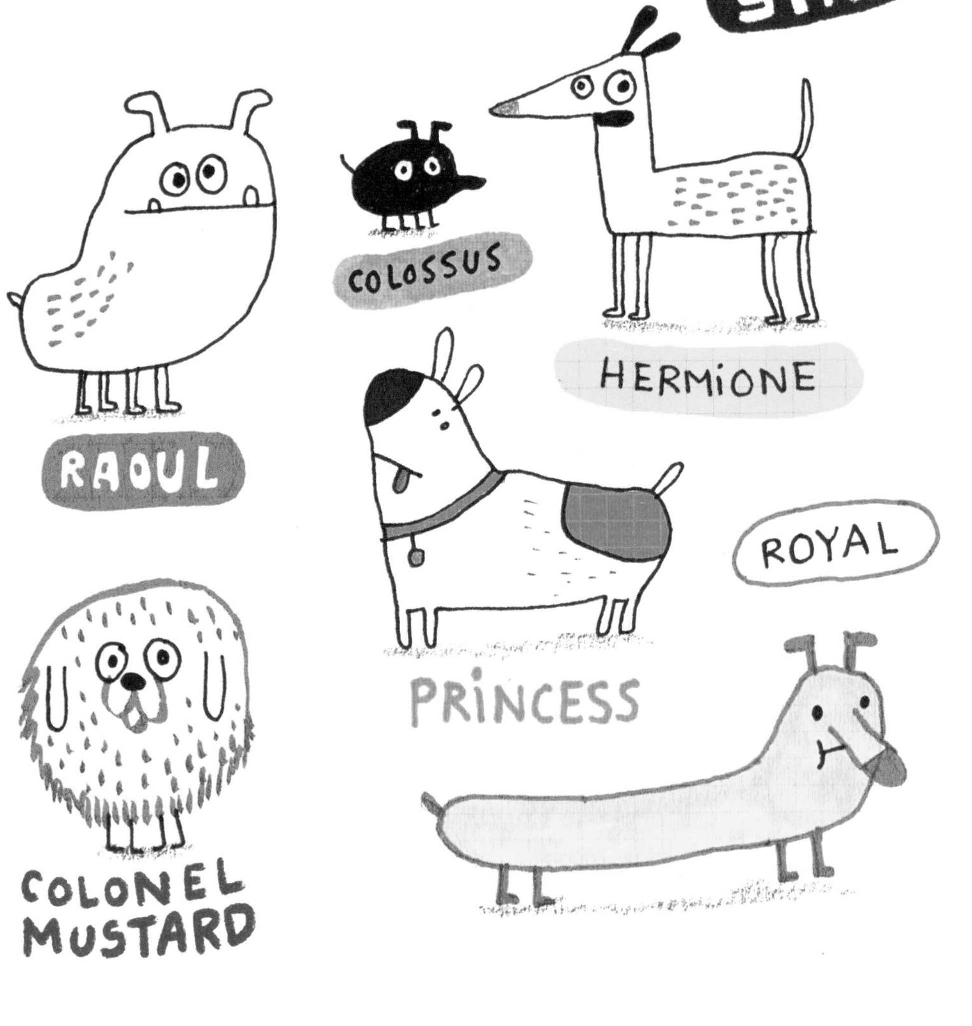

RAOUL
COLOSSUS
HERMIONE
PRINCESS
ROYAL
COLONEL MUSTARD

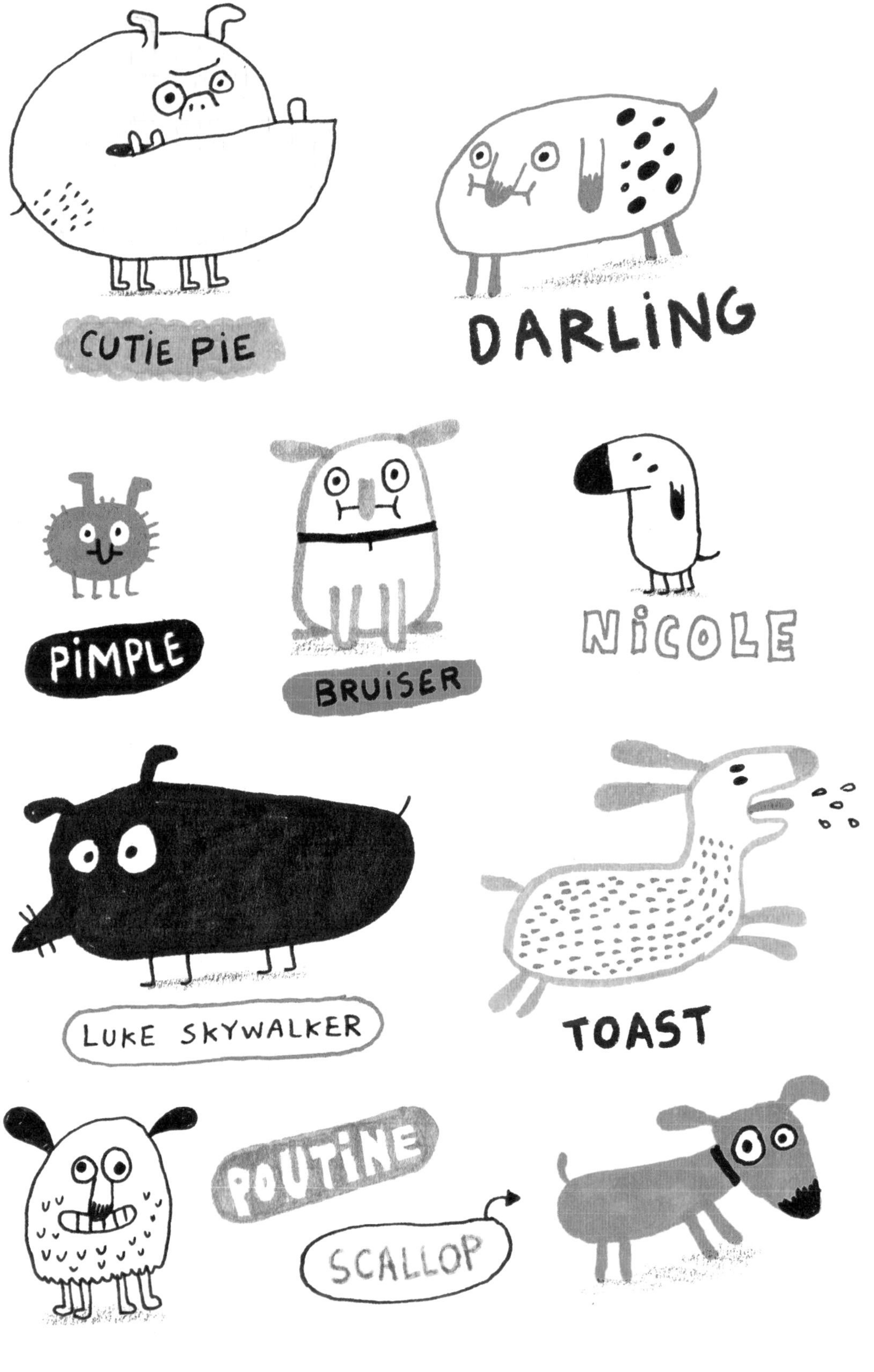
CUTIE PIE
DARLING
PIMPLE
BRUISER
NICOLE
LUKE SKYWALKER
TOAST
POUTINE
SCALLOP

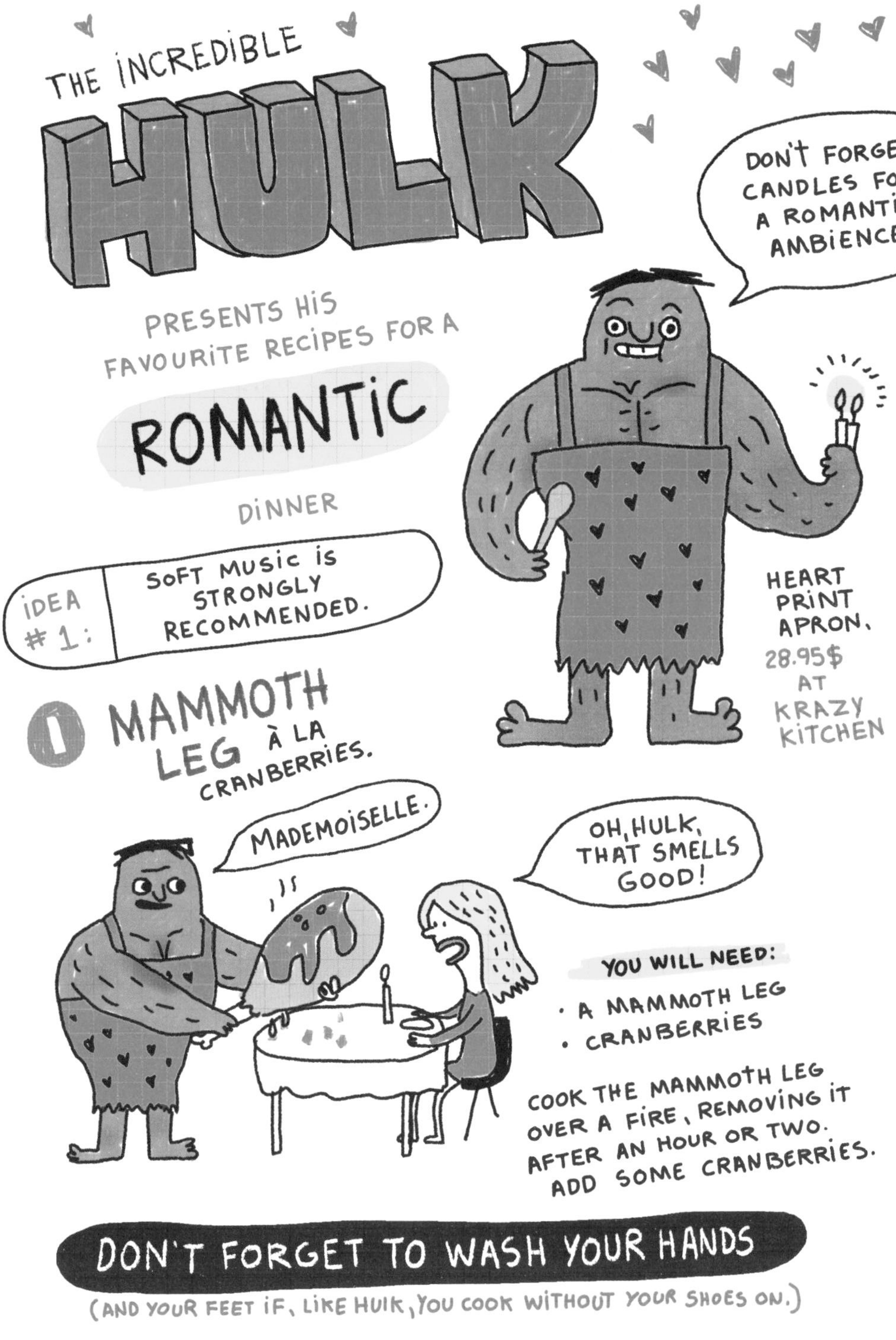
THE INCREDIBLE
HULK
PRESENTS HIS FAVOURITE RECIPES FOR A
ROMANTIC
DINNER
DON'T FORGET CANDLES FOR A ROMANTIC AMBIENCE.
IDEA #1:
SOFT MUSIC IS STRONGLY RECOMMENDED.
HEART PRINT APRON, 28.95$ AT KRAZY KITCHEN
1 MAMMOTH LEG À LA CRANBERRIES.
MADEMOISELLE.
OH, HULK, THAT SMELLS GOOD!
YOU WILL NEED:
· A MAMMOTH LEG
· CRANBERRIES
COOK THE MAMMOTH LEG OVER A FIRE, REMOVING IT AFTER AN HOUR OR TWO. ADD SOME CRANBERRIES.
DON'T FORGET TO WASH YOUR HANDS
(AND YOUR FEET IF, LIKE HULK, YOU COOK WITHOUT YOUR SHOES ON.)

2 GIANT PYRAMID OF OSTRICH EGGS IN VINEGAR

IT'S ALL IN THE PRESENTATION

YOU WILL NEED:

- A DOZEN OSTRICH EGGS
- VINEGAR
- A PIECE OF ASPARAGUS FOR DECORATION

BOIL THE EGGS, THEN LET THEM MARINATE FOR TWENTY-FOUR HOURS. TOP WITH A PIECE OF STEAMED ASPARAGUS BEFORE SERVING.

A TIP FROM THE HULK:

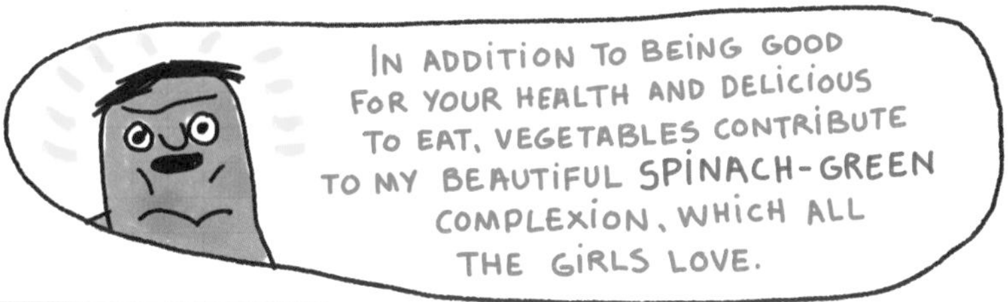

IN ADDITION TO BEING GOOD FOR YOUR HEALTH AND DELICIOUS TO EAT, VEGETABLES CONTRIBUTE TO MY BEAUTIFUL SPINACH-GREEN COMPLEXION, WHICH ALL THE GIRLS LOVE.

3 FOR DESSERT:

A DISH OF WILD BERRIES WITH CRÈME FRAÎCHE

THAT'S IT, I'M IN LOVE.

YOU WILL NEED:

- BERRIES
- CRÈME FRAÎCHE
- PLATE

MIX THE FRUIT, THE PLATE, AND THE CRÈME FRAÎCHE, AND VOILA!

A TIP: YOU CAN ALSO ADD SPIDERS, BUT IT MIGHT TASTE WEIRD.

IMAGINARY STRONG MEN

(UH, NO, UNFORTUNATELY THEY AREN'T REAL)

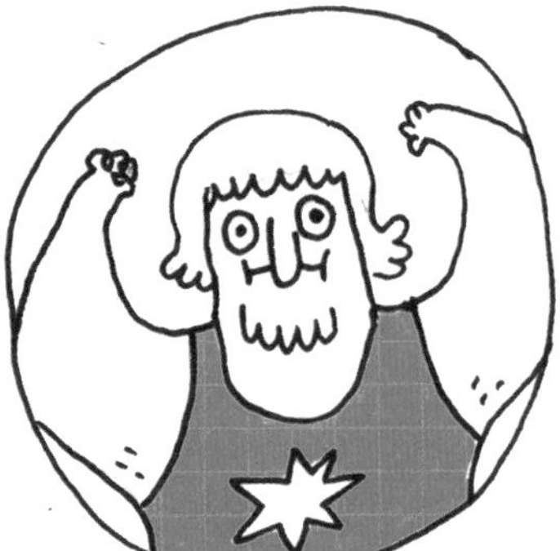

ANATOLE KLOPS

can lift a fridge and transport it twenty kilometres

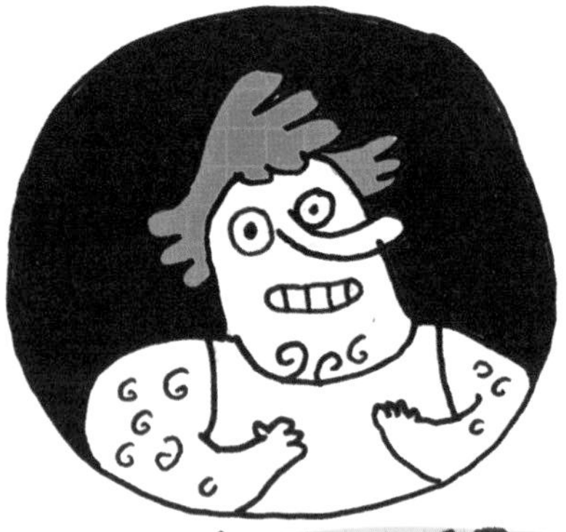

KLOPPI MOGGZ

can scale Everest with a cow in his backpack

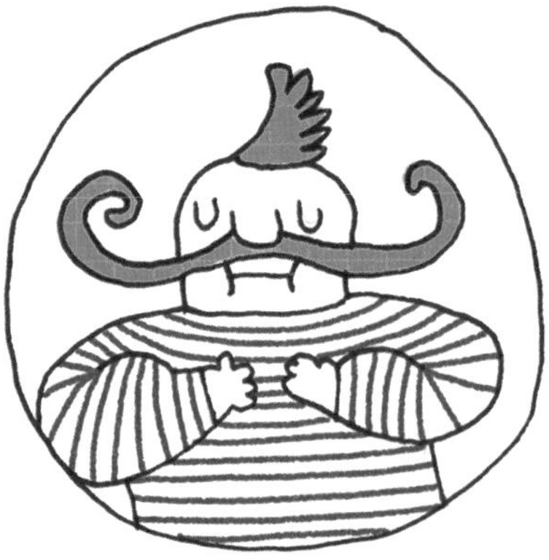

MOMO LACAISSE

can pull a tank with his moustache

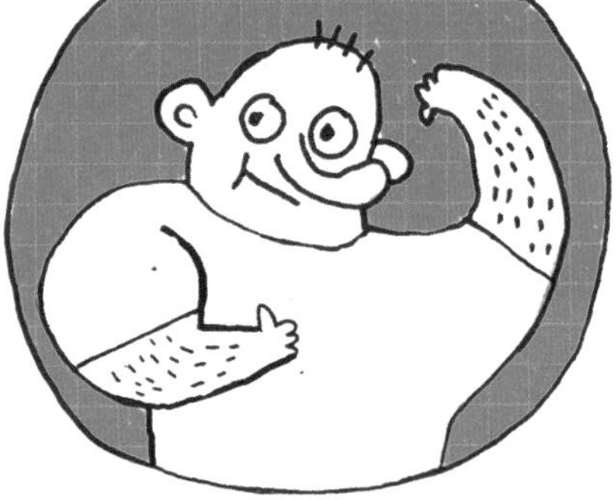

FRITON LABINE

can lift a boat full of sand with his nose

STRONG WOMEN

(ALSO IMAGINARY)

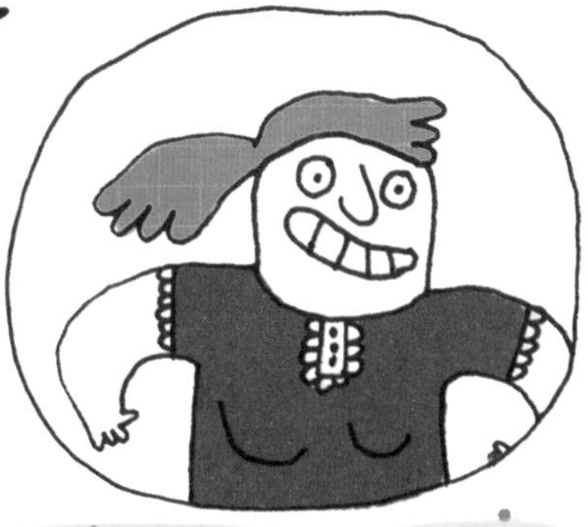

MIFLETTE ZOUPI
can carry two tons of potatoes in her purse

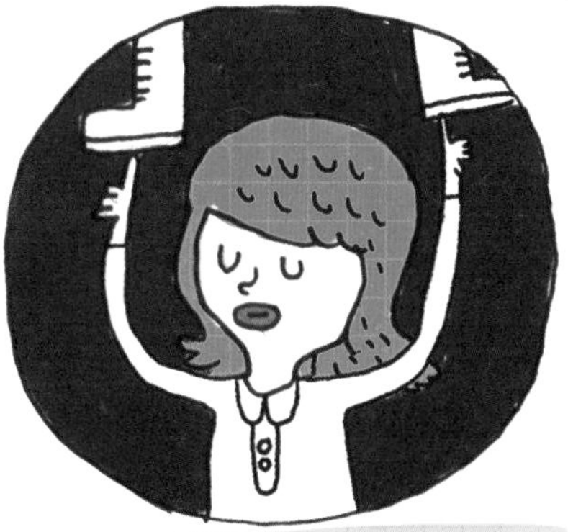

BRETTA HOMS
can lift Kloppi Moggz and Friton Labine with her pinkies

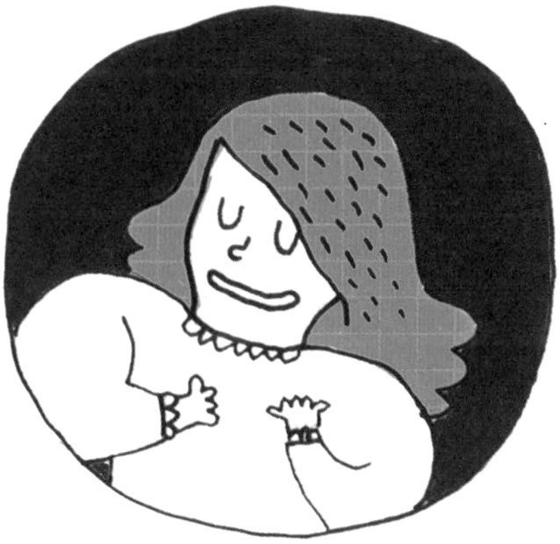

KABOSH BIBOSH
can tightrope walk with a tractor balanced on her head

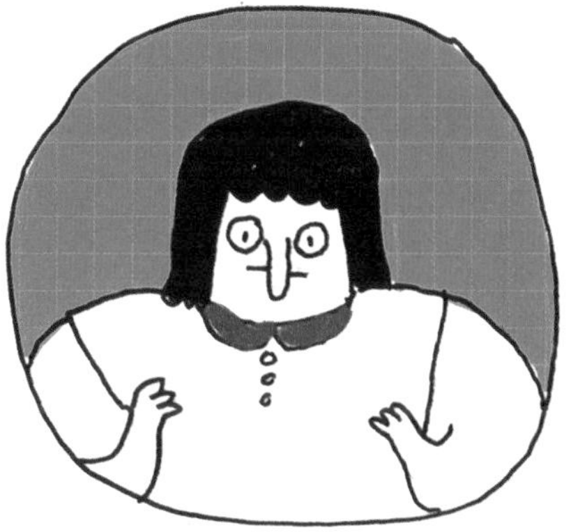

SMURTA FUNZX
can throw an oil tanker over another oil tanker

BIZARRE AND RIDICULOUS CREATURES

that pop into my mind when I'm daydreaming:

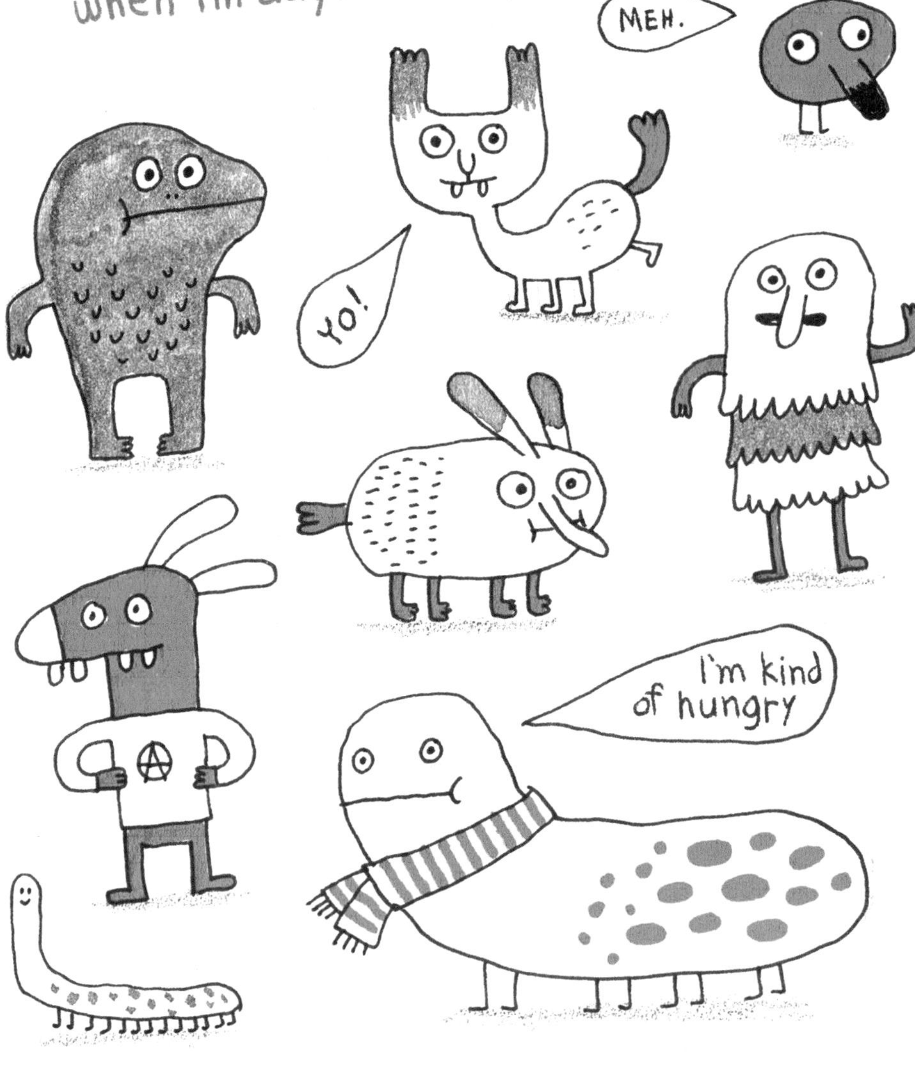
MEH.
YO!
I'm kind of hungry

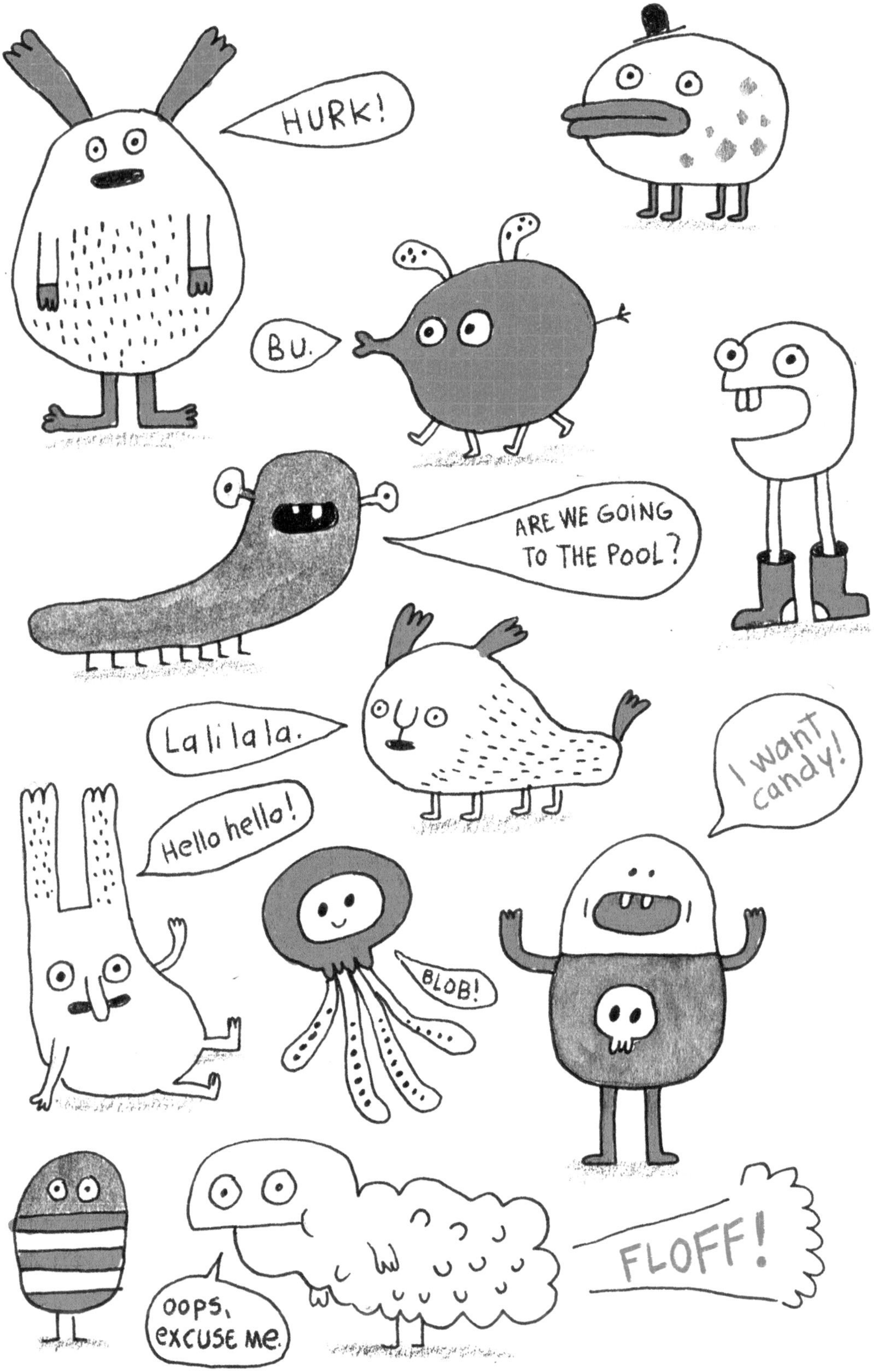
HURK!
BU.
ARE WE GOING TO THE POOL?
La li la la.
I want candy!
Hello hello!
BLOB!
oops, excuse me.
FLOFF!

Michael is a sweetheart.
He could spend all his time
just watching cars go by
and sleeping in the tall grass.

He feeds on cattails and
dandelion buds.

He is sometimes found outside
behind restaurants because he
likes the smell of French fries.

I do too.

MICHAEL

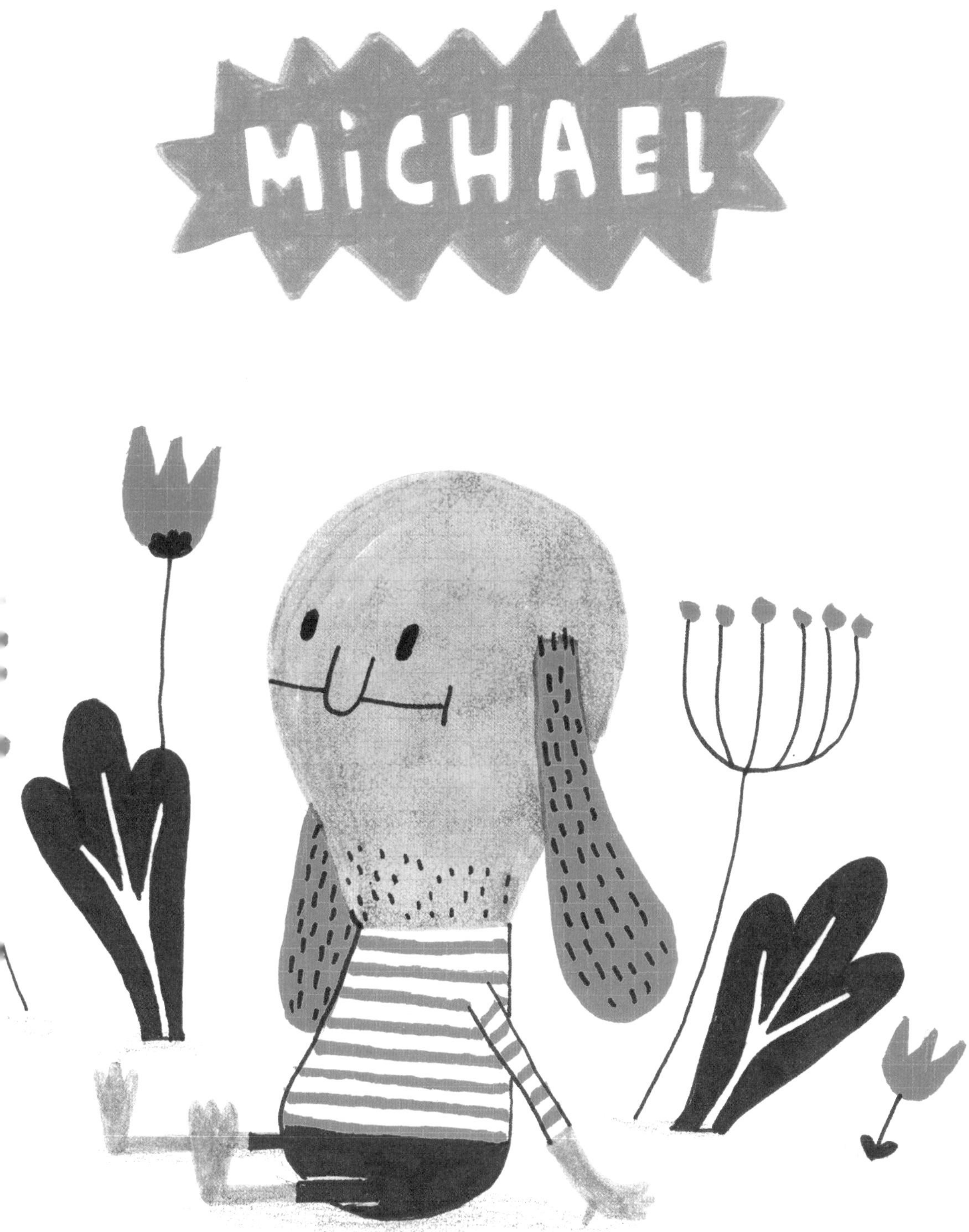

Are you also fascinated by creatures that live underground? Here are a few species that you've probably never seen. They live underneath my garden. You remember, my weird garden? I talked about it earlier.

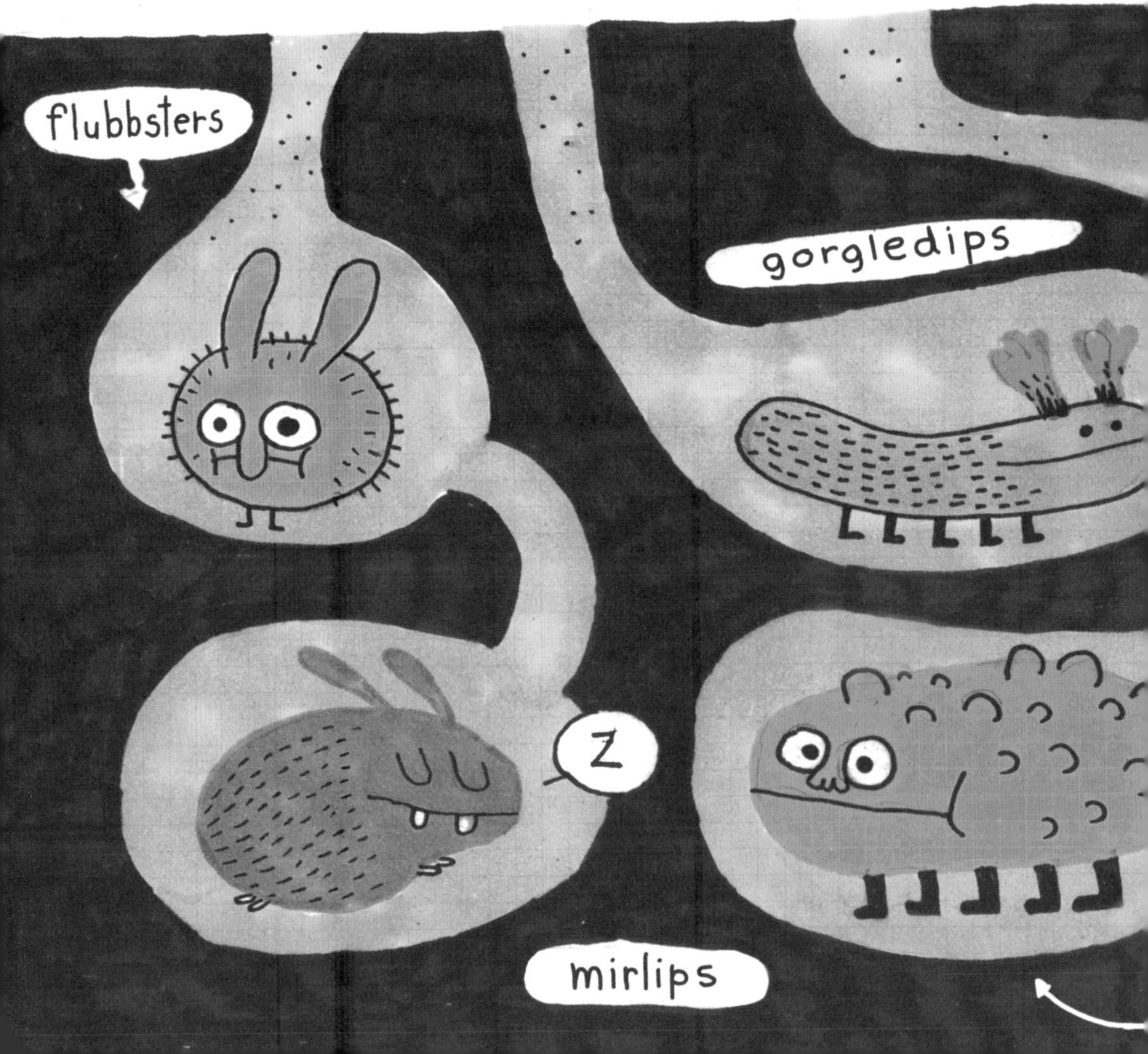
flubbsters
gorgledips
Z
mirlips

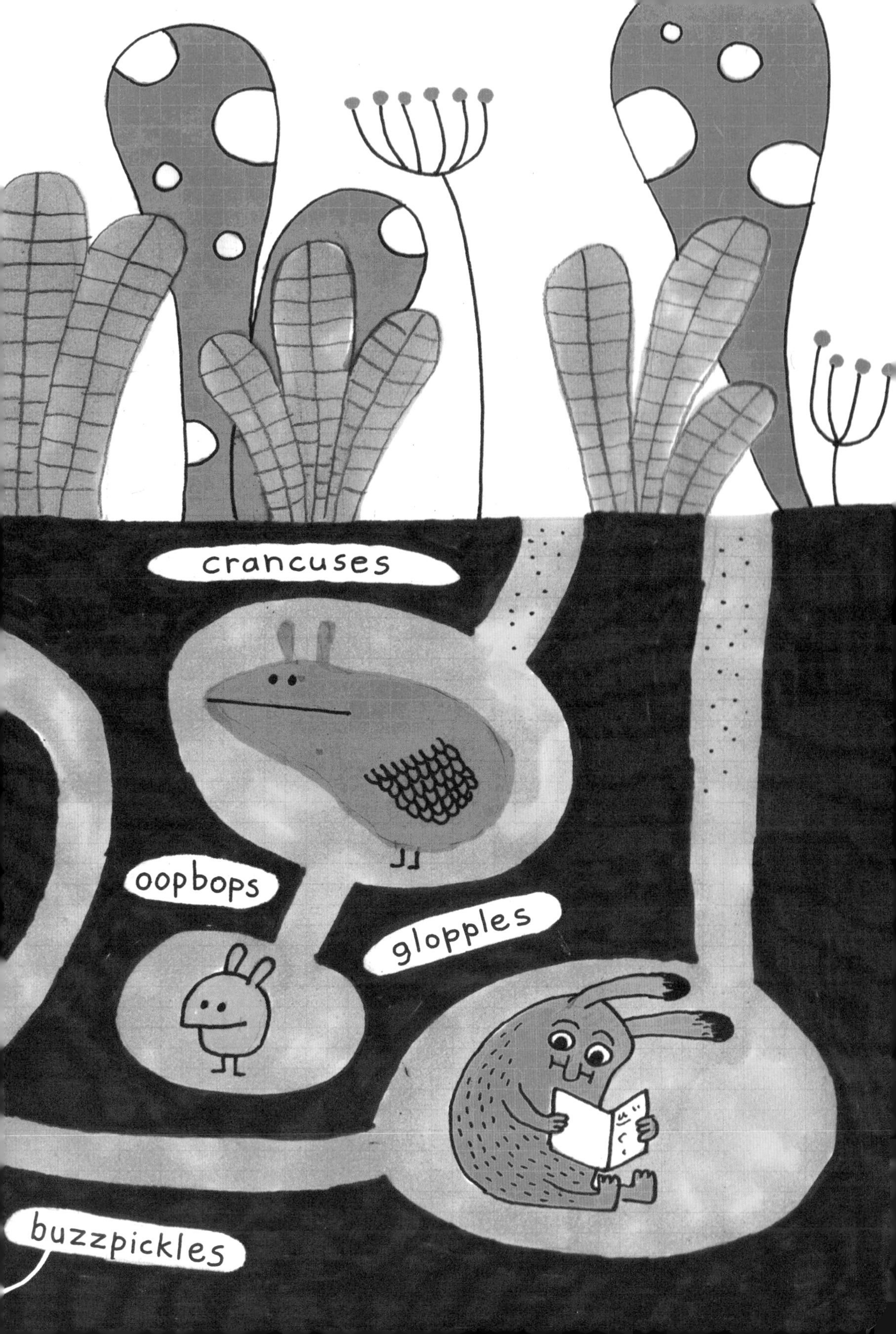
crancuses
oopbops
glopples
buzzpickles

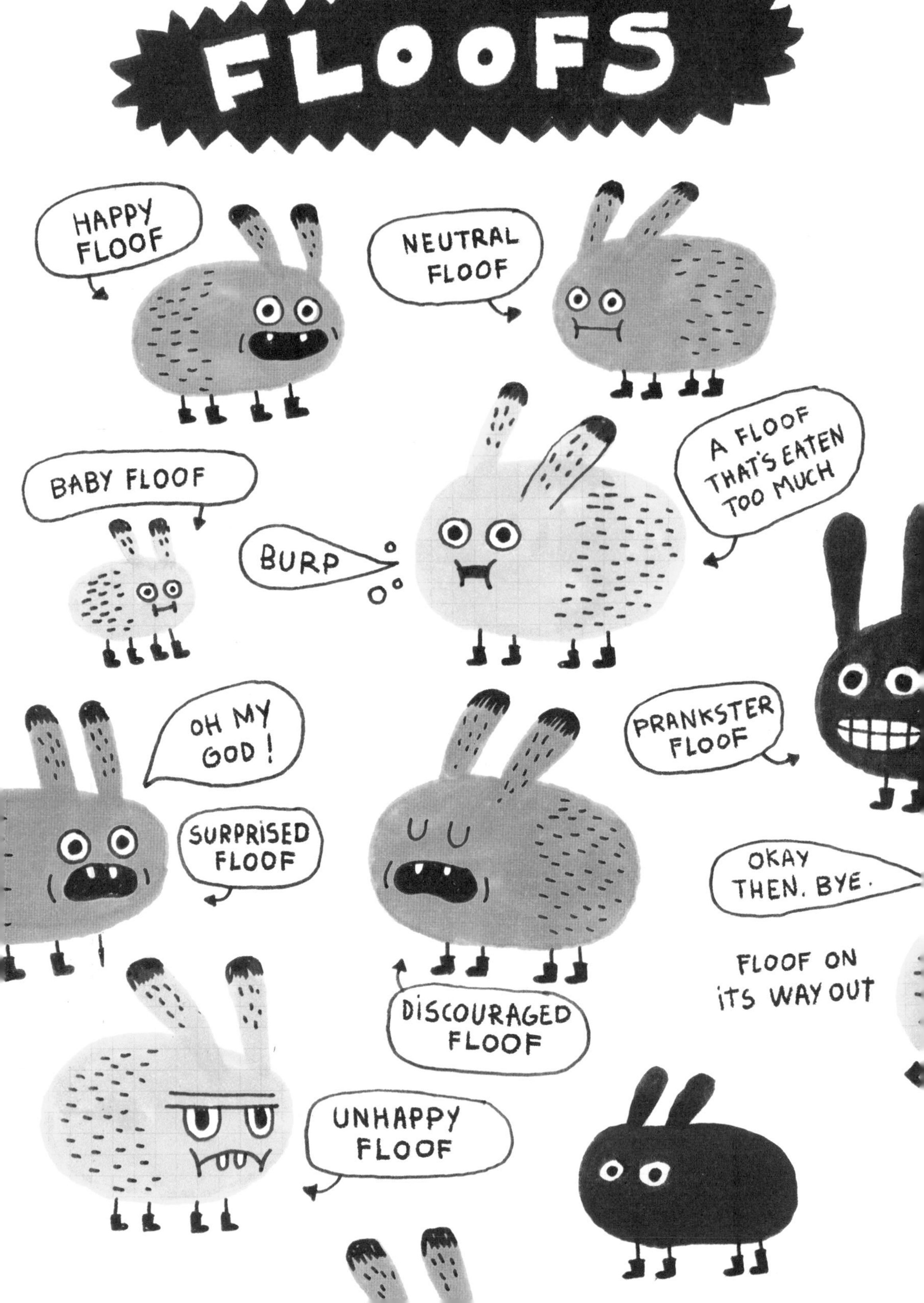
FLOOFS
HAPPY FLOOF
NEUTRAL FLOOF
BABY FLOOF
A FLOOF THAT'S EATEN TOO MUCH
BURP
OH MY GOD!
PRANKSTER FLOOF
SURPRISED FLOOF
OKAY THEN. BYE.
FLOOF ON ITS WAY OUT
DISCOURAGED FLOOF
UNHAPPY FLOOF

Floofs are like bunnies, but they
wear boots. And bite. Really hard!
Believe me. I still have a bandage
on my right hand from when
I tried to tickle one of them.
Bad idea.

Floofs are really good at working
in teams. They often win soccer
games and spelling bees.

What else can I tell you about floofs?
They never clean up their rooms.
They can be trained to pee in the
toilet. You should NEVER give
them coffee or sit on them.
That's about it.

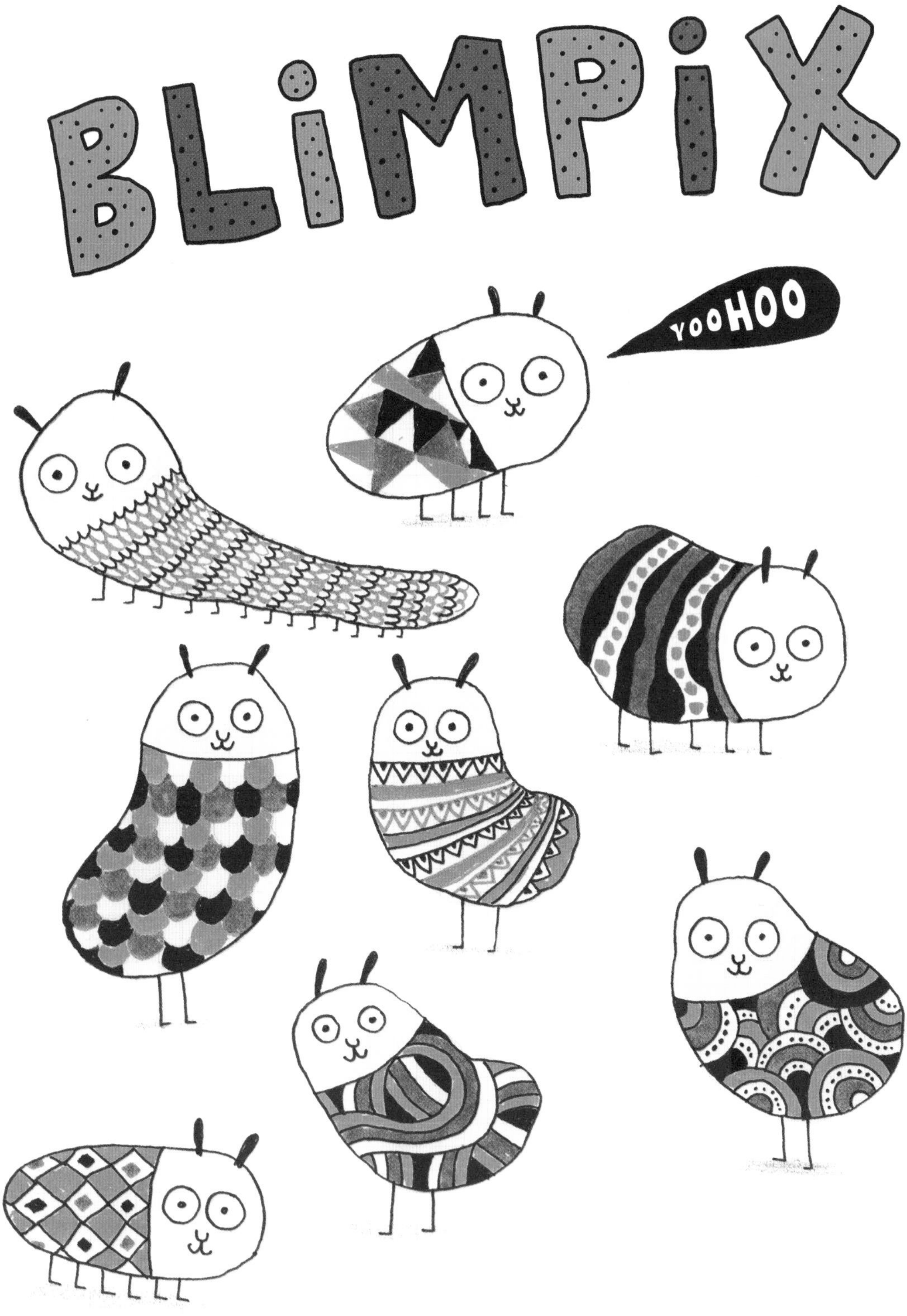
BLIMPIX
YOOHOO

Blimpix are little creatures who live in groups in the desert. They live principally on cactus juice, but they like it if you give them chocolate muffins every now and again.

They often argue amongst themselves and sometimes fight. It's not nice to see. They throw rocks and pebbles while yelling insults.

When they've had enough, they make a hole in the sand and take a nap.

In general, they're in a much better mood after they've napped.

This is

MAURICE,

the cousin of Bernard.
You remember, the kind of
FOX - RABBIT?

Maurice is very rarely
seen because he's
extremely timid. You
can coax him out
with chocolate
doughnuts
though.

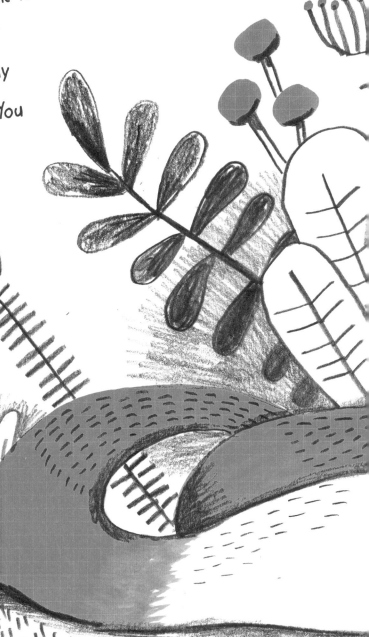

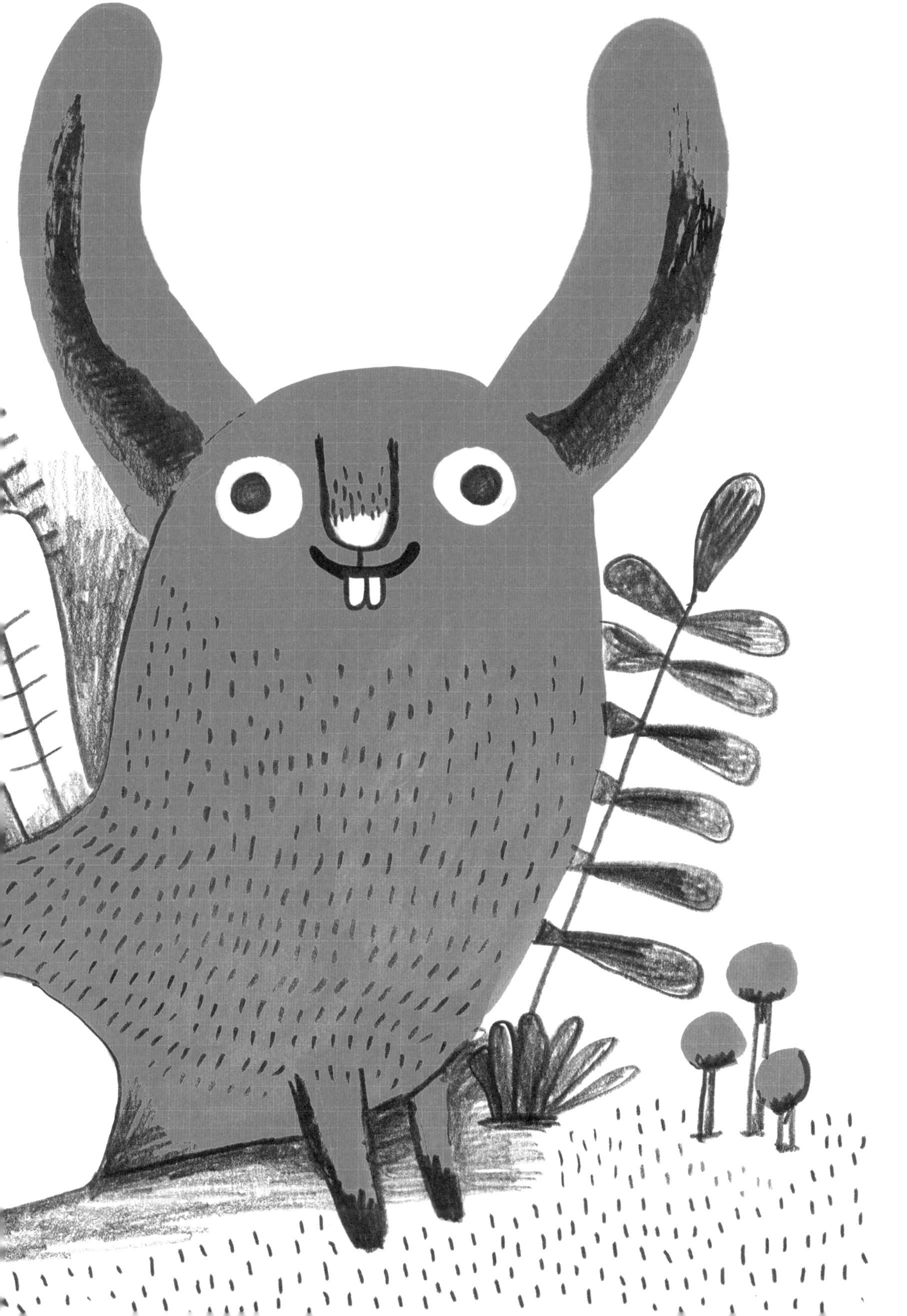

FOXES

Seriously, there's nothing cuter than foxes, don't you agree? I don't know anyone who doesn't like foxes. When I draw foxes and share the drawings on the internet, everyone goes crazy.

I NEED a tame fox in my life. Or a dog that looks exactly like a fox. Or a hamster that looks like a fox. Or a goldfish that looks like a fox. But in the meantime, I just draw them.

The one below on the right is saying "Hello" to you in arabic. It's pronounced "As-salamu Alaykum."

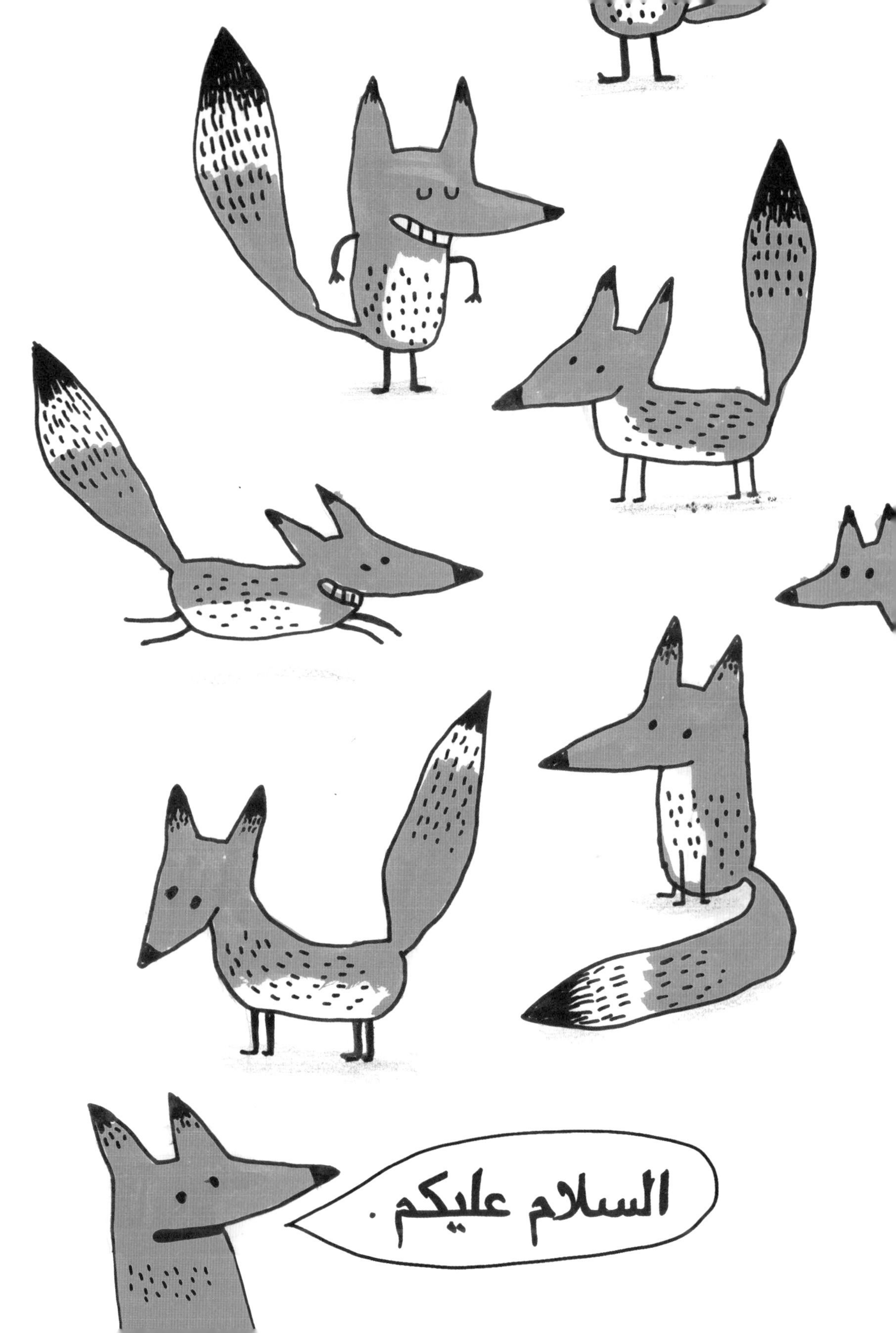
السلام عليكم.

Okay, you might be saying: "It's not fair, Elise Gravel said that she draws anything, anyhow, but her drawings aren't that bad!"

That, my friend, is because I cheated a little. I chose the most beautiful drawings from my black notebook to put in this collection.

But in reality, I SWEAR to you that I do a lot of ugly drawings. Sometimes, I do such ugly drawings that I feel like breaking my pencil. Yes indeed! It's the absolute truth! Here, look, I made a whole page of ugly drawings to prove it's okay and that it's not the end of the world.

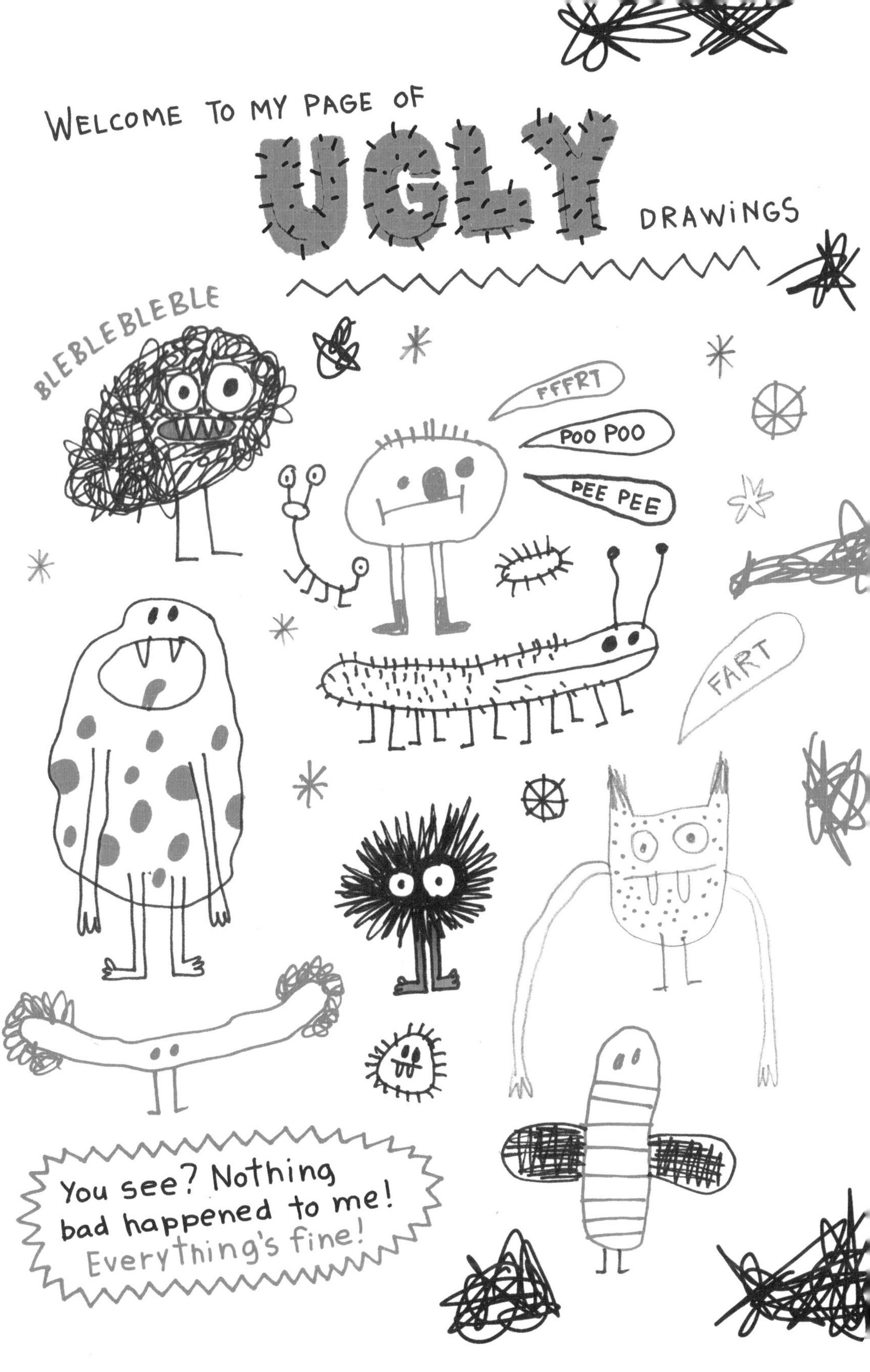
WELCOME TO MY PAGE OF
UGLY
DRAWINGS
BLEBLEBLEBLE
FFFRT
POO POO
PEE PEE
FART
You see? Nothing bad happened to me! Everything's fine!

Other imaginary friends:

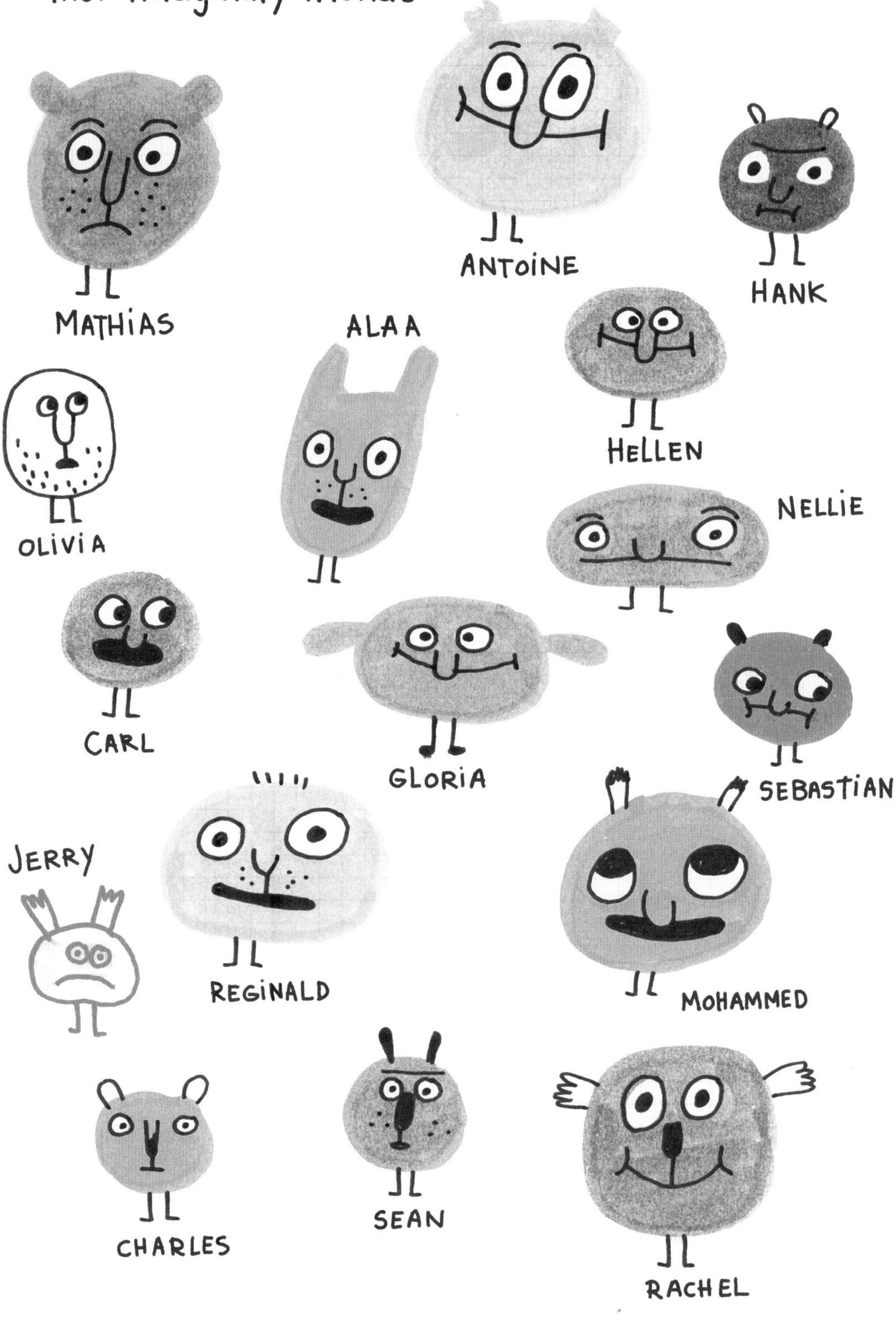
MATHIAS
ANTOINE
HANK
ALAA
HELLEN
OLIVIA
NELLIE
CARL
GLORIA
SEBASTIAN
JERRY
REGINALD
MOHAMMED
CHARLES
SEAN
RACHEL

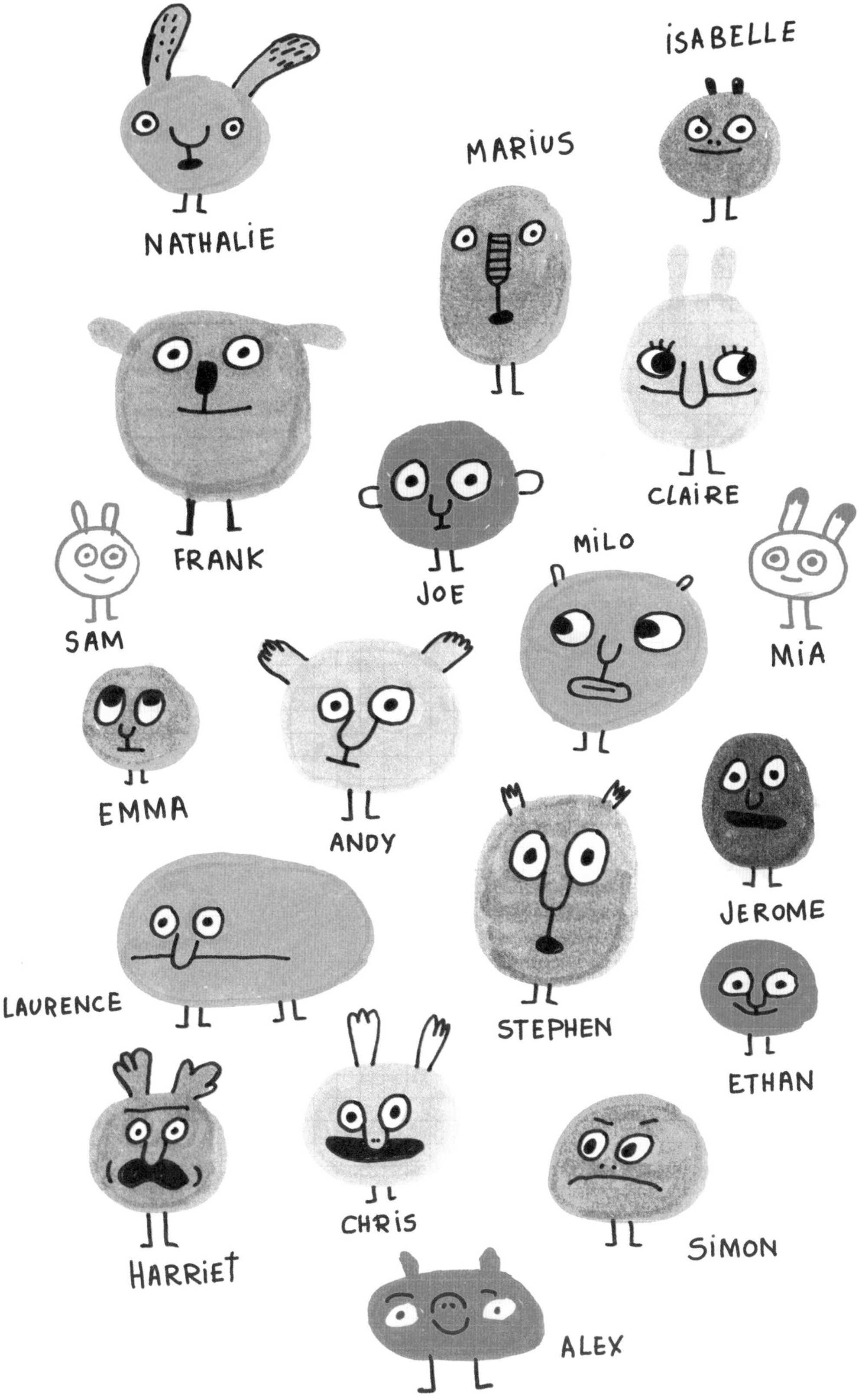
NATHALIE
MARIUS
ISABELLE
FRANK
CLAIRE
JOE
SAM
MILO
MIA
EMMA
ANDY
JEROME
LAURENCE
STEPHEN
ETHAN
HARRIET
CHRIS
SIMON
ALEX

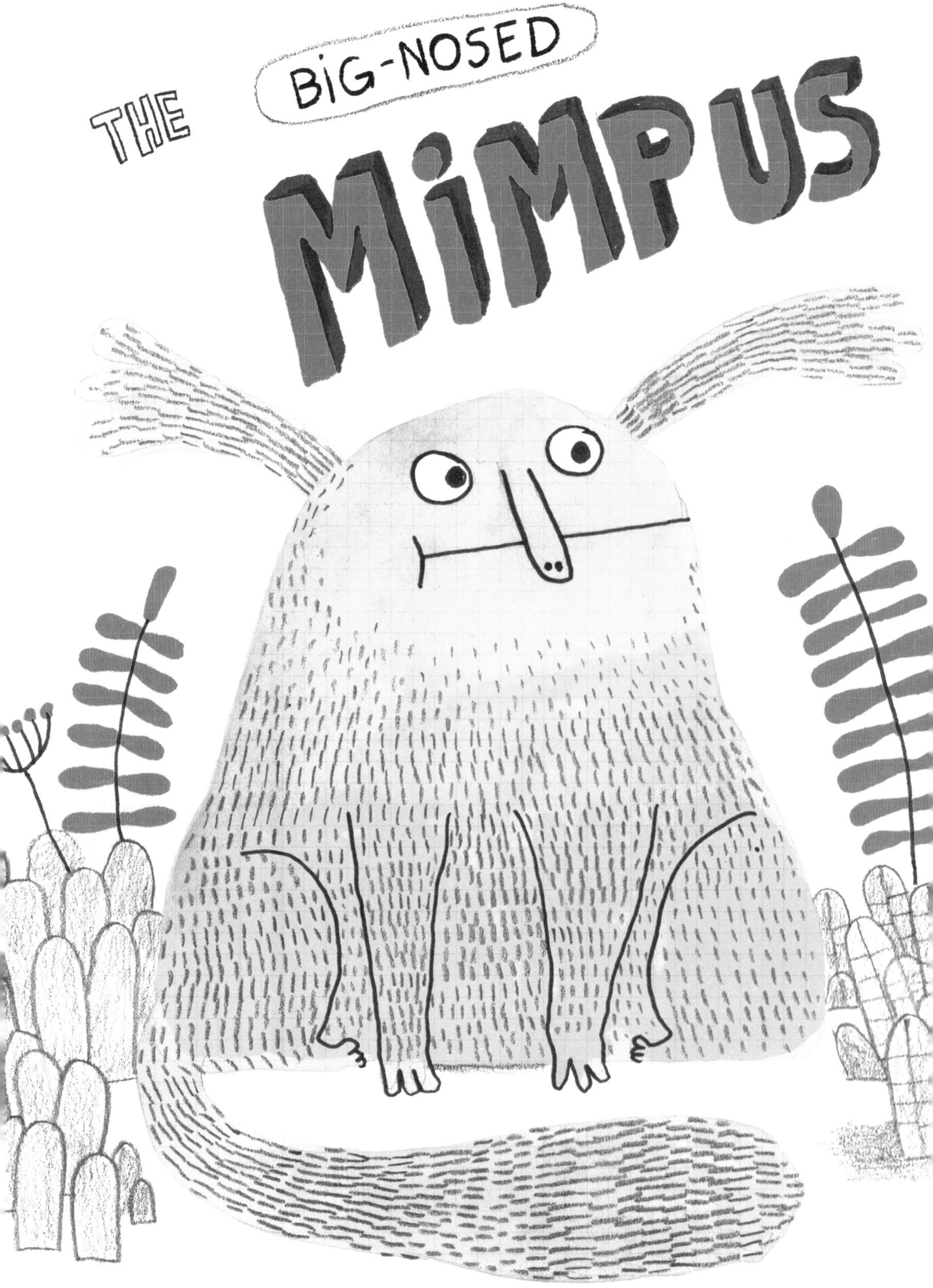
THE
BIG-NOSED
MIMPUS

The big-nosed mimpus is a small North American mammal. It's pretty calm, except when something smells bad—then it gets into a terrible rage. Otherwise, it's a good companion. It makes bracelets out of fern while whistling through its large nostrils. It's very afraid of people with moustaches and is a huge fan of Michael Jackson.

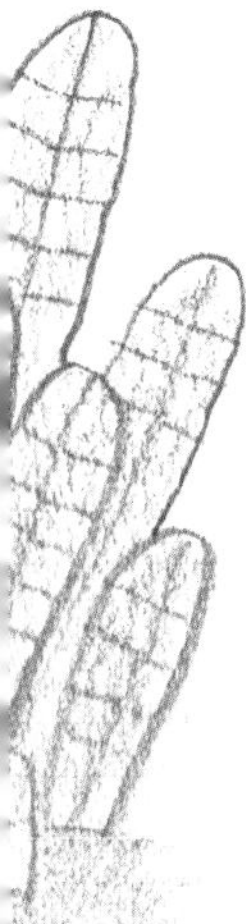

WEiRD COOL! WOW!

ANiMALS THAT REALLY EXiST!

THEY'RE AS WEiRD AS MY MONSTERS, BUT I DiDN'T iNVENT THEM! I FiND THEM iNCREDiBLY CUTE AND WANT TO ADOPT ALL OF THEM. DON'T YOU?

GiMME A KiSS?

ELiJAH

THE RED-LiPPED BATFiSH

YO!

CHRiSTOPHER

THE DUMBO OCTOPUS (MY FAVOURiTE CREATURE iN THE WORLD)

Hiiiiiiiiii.

ABiGAiL

THE EASTERN LONG-NECKED TURTLE, WHO LiVES iN AUSTRALiA

I WANT A KISS TOO.

NOT ME.

GROSS.

SAMUEL

A SNAKEHEAD FISH
WHO HAS A VERY
FRIENDLY FACE.

ROSALIE

THE STAR-NOSED MOLE,
WHO HAS A VERY,
UMM...STAR-SHAPED
NOSE.

GABRIEL

THE YETI CRAB,
WHO IS REALLY
TOO CUTE!

HEY, I'M A FAN
OF NUDISM,
THAT'S ALL.

CHARLES

THE NAKED MOLE-RAT,
WHO SHOULD REALLY
WEAR UNDERPANTS.
IT WOULD BE MORE POLITE.

I CAN'T TALK,
I DON'T HAVE
A MOUTH. *

LILLIAN

THE SEA PIG,
WHO LOOKS LIKE A BIG
BALL OF BUBBLE GUM
WITH LOTS OF
TENTACLES.

* FACT COMPLETELY
MADE UP BY THE AUTHOR

I drew a hamster just for you.
His name is

He likes to hide in toilet paper
tubes. He also likes to stuff his
cheeks with corn kernels. He
digs tunnels in sawdust and
gallops all night on his hamster
wheel, pretending to be a
wild horse.

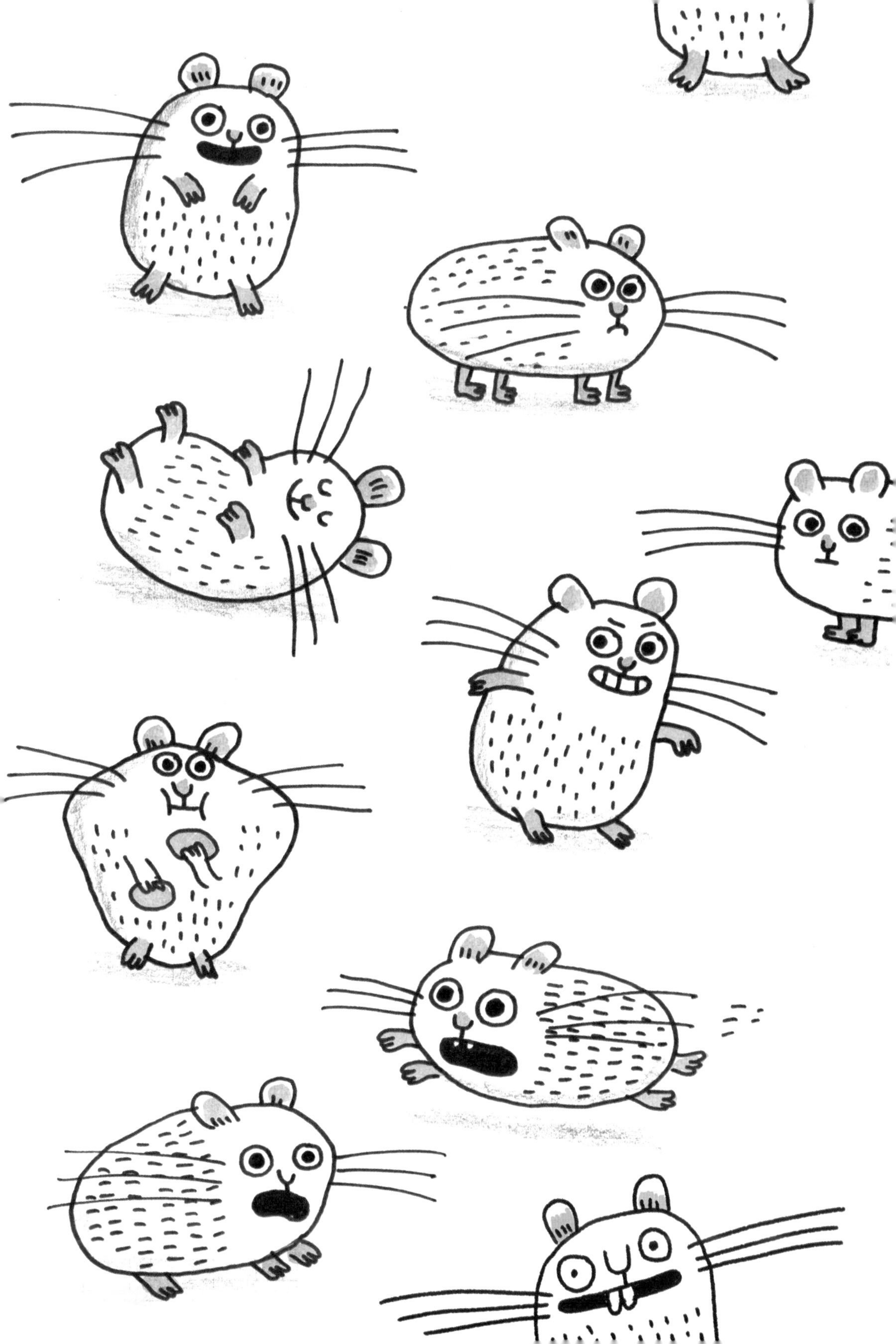

THE PERFUME-FOOTED WOMPUS

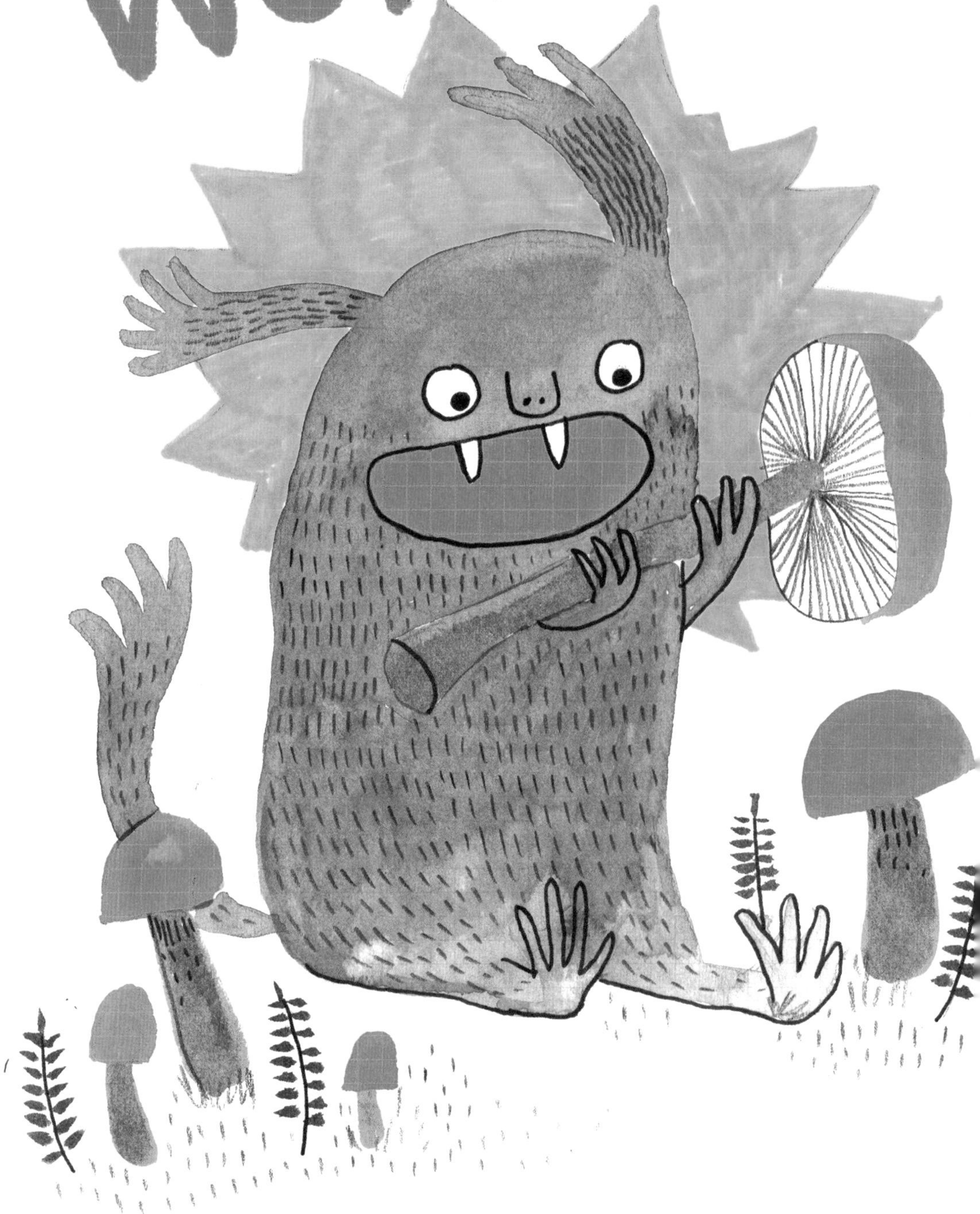

The perfume-footed wompus
is a small forest monster, a close
cousin to the squirrel. He feeds on
mushrooms and, on special occasions,
fries with ketchup. He communicates
with a little sharp cry that sounds
like an angry baby.

His feet give off a powerful
odour that smells like my
aunt Pierrette's perfume,
Fleur d'Oubli, which is
available in stores for
$79 a bottle.

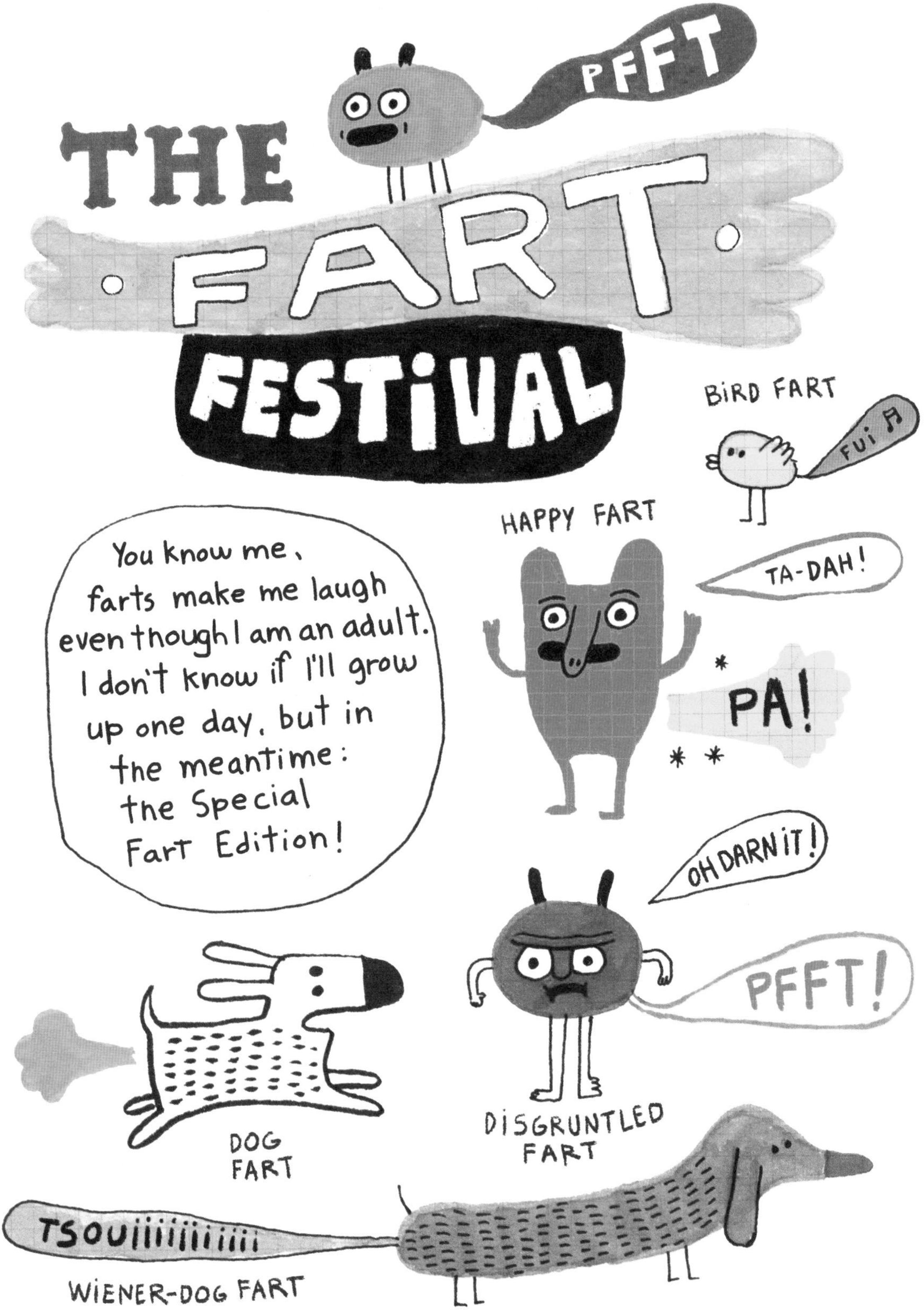

THE FART FESTIVAL
PFFT
You know me, farts make me laugh even though I am an adult. I don't know if I'll grow up one day, but in the meantime: the Special Fart Edition!
BIRD FART
FUi ♫
HAPPY FART
TA-DAH!
PA!
OH DARN IT!
PFFT!
DISGRUNTLED FART
DOG FART
TSOUiiiiiiiiiii
WIENER-DOG FART

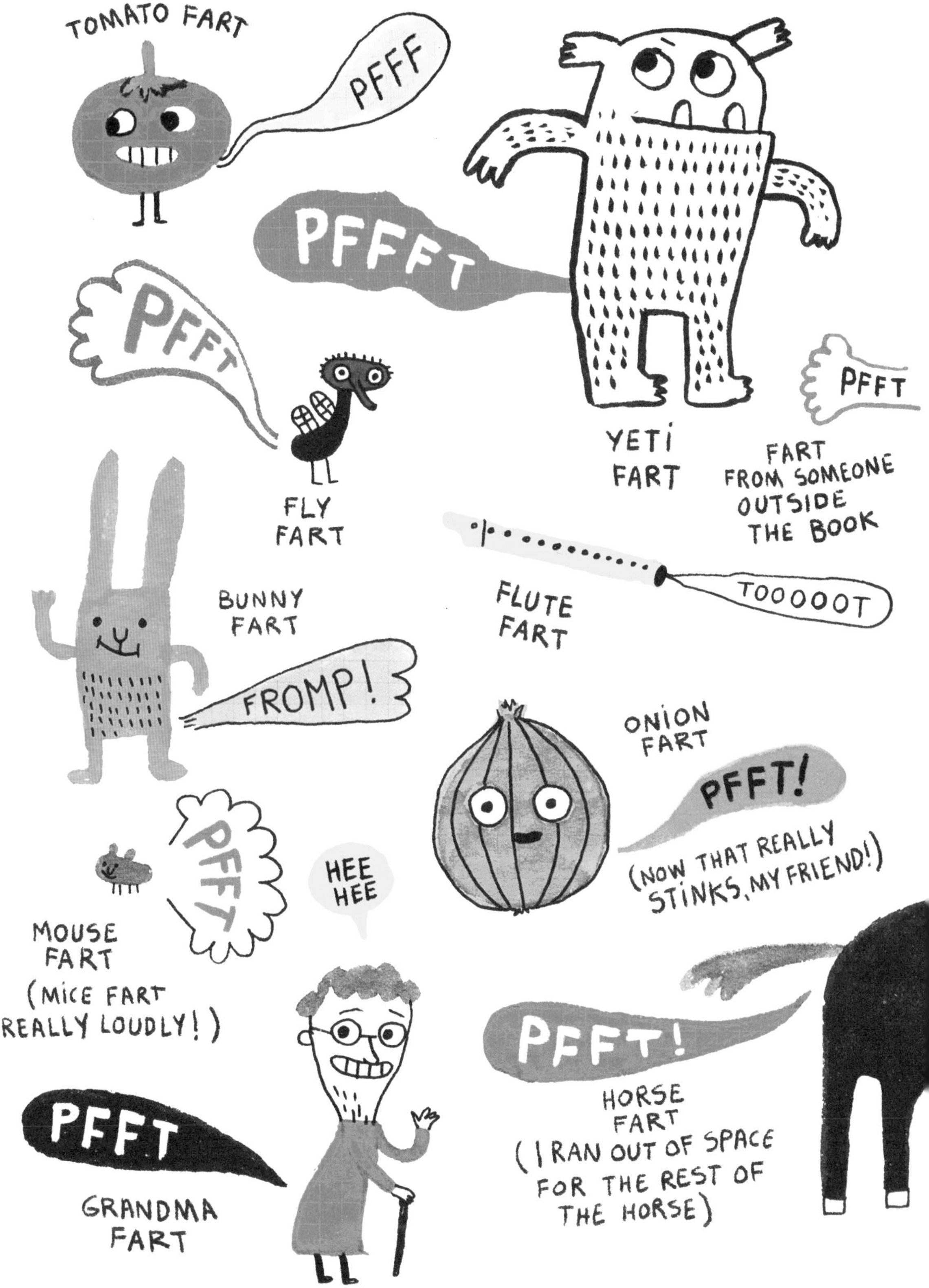

TOMATO FART
PFFF
PFFFT
PFFFT
YETI FART
PFFT
FART FROM SOMEONE OUTSIDE THE BOOK
FLY FART
BUNNY FART
FROMP!
FLUTE FART
TOOOOOT
ONION FART
PFFT!
(NOW THAT REALLY STINKS, MY FRIEND!)
PFFT
HEE HEE
MOUSE FART
(MICE FART REALLY LOUDLY!)
PFFT!
HORSE FART
(I RAN OUT OF SPACE FOR THE REST OF THE HORSE)
PFFT
GRANDMA FART

THE  **POCKLES**

Pockles live in drawers in human houses. They keep very quiet, waiting until we leave for school or work and then—BAM! It's a party.

They fill the bathtub all the way to the top and add lots of peach-scented bubble bath. They put on really loud music and dance naked in the kitchen, getting soap bubbles everywhere. They eat all our chocolate cookies, make faces at our neighbours, and go pee on the hall rug.

Seriously, pockles.
You're annoying.

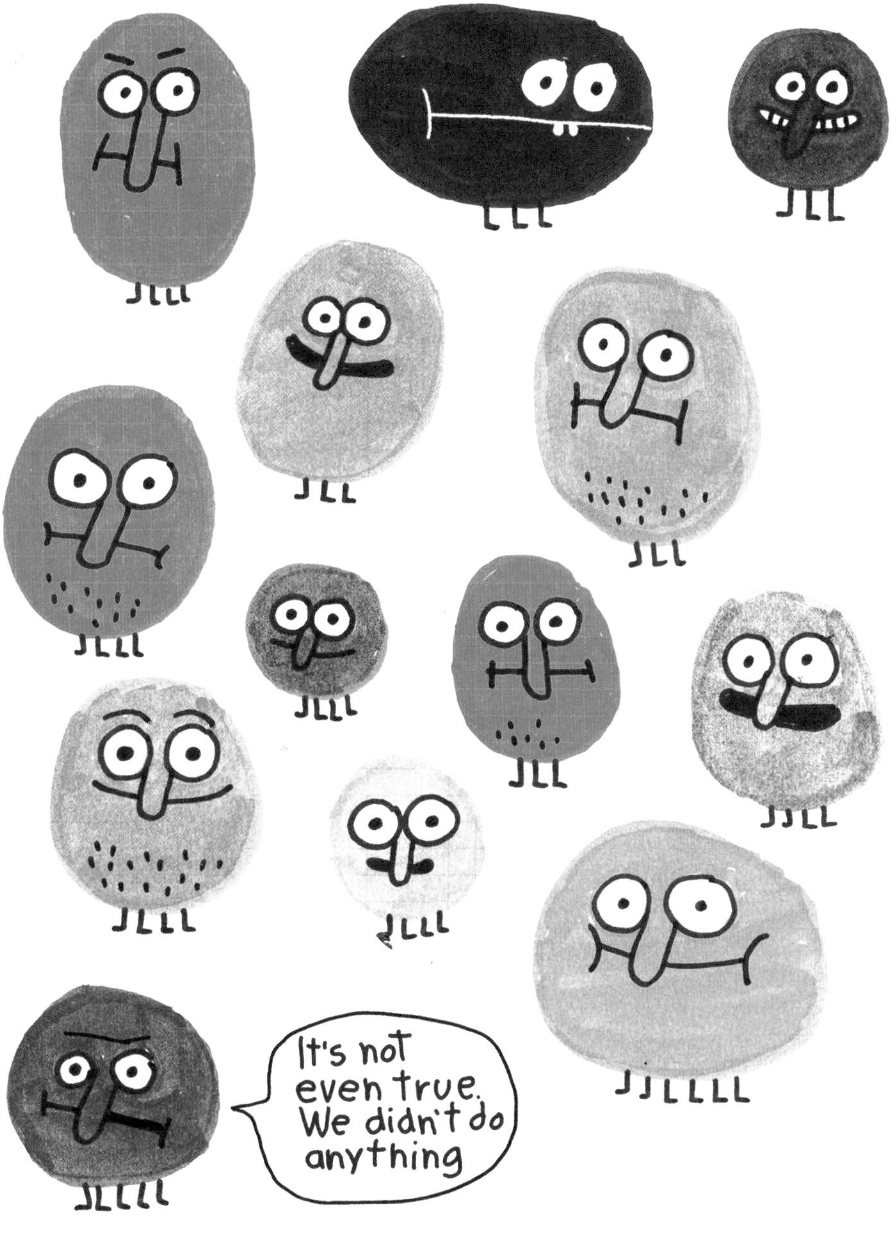
It's not even true. We didn't do anything

Some jellyfish speaking

ITALIAN.

Because they're pretty (both the jellyfish and the Italian).

Jellyfish in Italian =

MEDUSA.

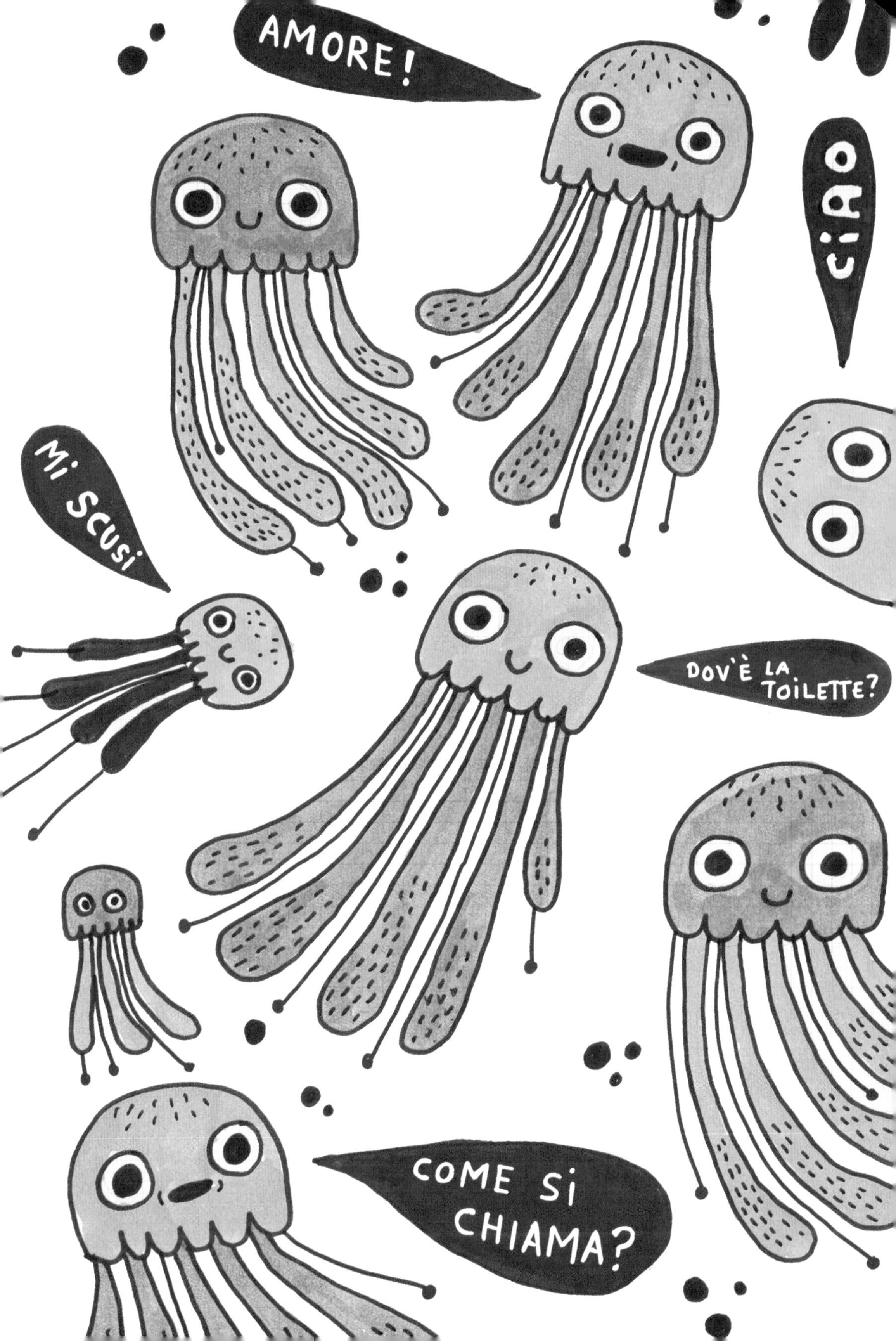
AMORE!
CIAO
Mi Scusi
DOV'È LA TOILETTE?
COME Si CHIAMA?

So, we're already at the end of my little black notebook.

What'll we do now?

Well...

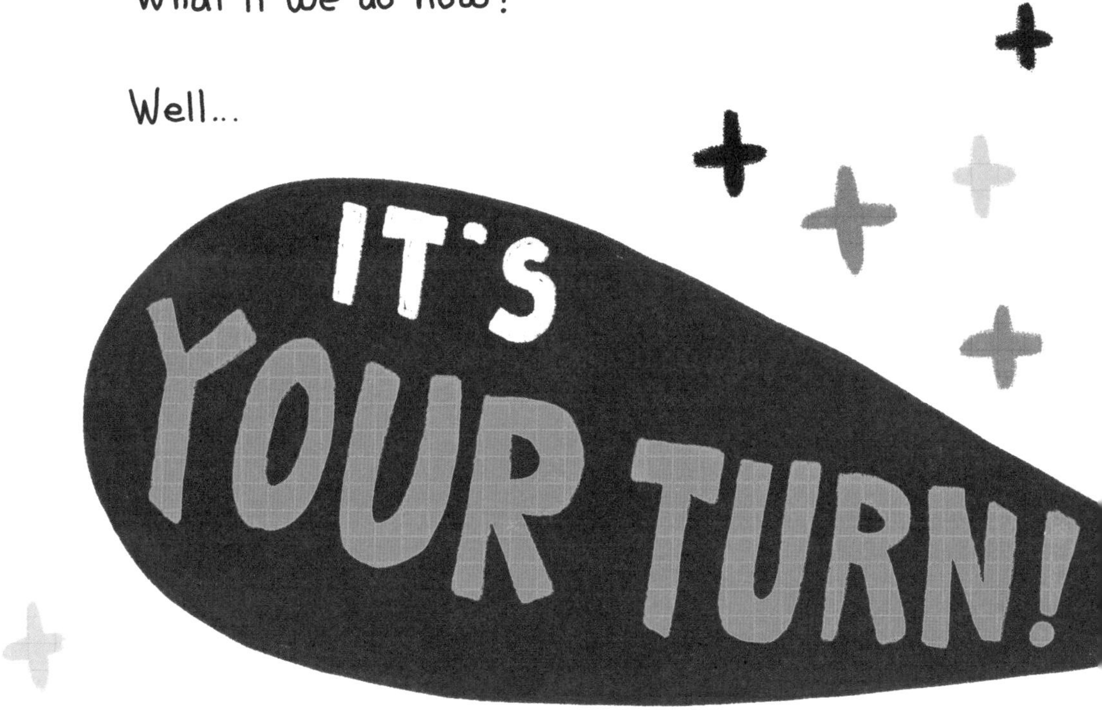
IT'S
YOUR TURN!

You don't have a little black notebook? You can use one that's red, blue, or pink, with a unicorn on the cover, or Stars Wars, or kittens. I hope that you'll have as much fun as I do drawing in it. Because really, that's the only thing that matters.

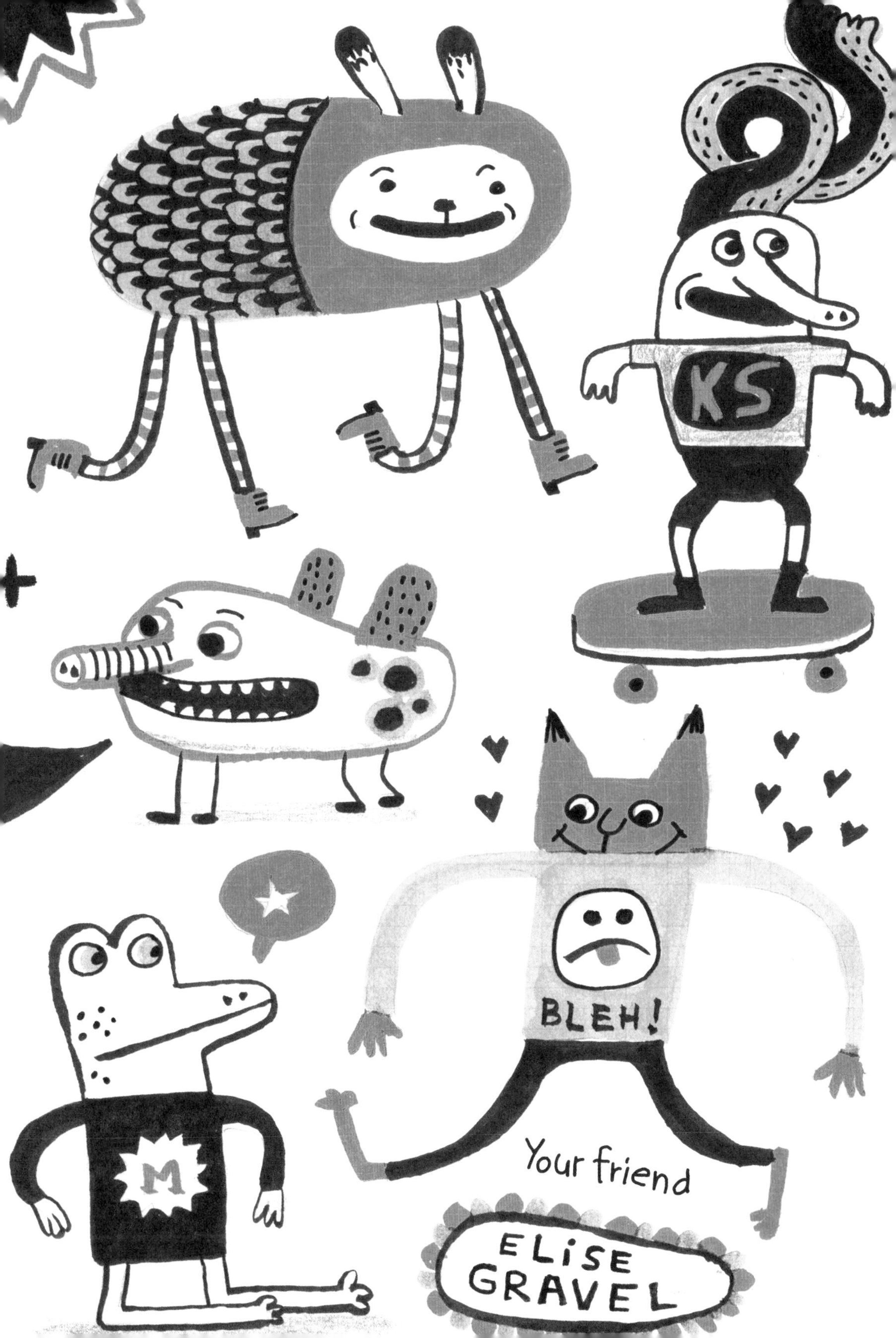
KS
BLEH!
M
Your friend
ELISE GRAVEL

Things you can  DRAW IN YOUR BOOK:

PIRATES

SPIDERS

YOUR FAVORITE FOODS

 STINKY STUFF

GROSS CREATURES

 SPACE AND SPACESHIPS

PRINCESSES

WHAT YOU'D LIKE TO FIND ON A DESERT ISLAND

BUTTERFLIES

THE PEOPLE YOU LOVE

WEIRD MACHINES

FUNNY CLOTHES

HORSES

THINGS WE COULD FIND UNDER THE  SEA

 MONKEYS

BATS

EVIL GUYS

 A MAZE

A PLAN OF YOUR DREAM HOUSE

FUNNY RECIPES

BABIES

 FLOWERS

FISH

THE COOLEST TOY STORE EVER!

CASTLES

If Found... Please Return to Elise Gravel copyright © 2017 Elise Gravel.
Translation copyright © 2017 Shira Adriance. Lettering © 2017 Richard Suicide.
All rights reserved. No part of this book (except small portions for review
purposes) may be reproduced in any form without written permission from
Elise Gravel or Drawn & Quarterly. Originally published by 400 coups.

drawnandquarterly.com | elisegravel.com

First English edition: June 2017 | Printed in China
10 9 8 7 6 5 4 3 2 1

Library and Archives Canada Cataloguing in Publication
Gravel, Élise [N'importe quoi! English] If Found... Please Return to Elise Gravel.
Translation of: N'importe quoi!
ISBN 978-1-77046-278-6 (hardback)
    1. Comics (Graphic works). I. Adriance, Shira, translator
II. Title. III. Title: N'importe quoi! English.
PN6733. G72N5513 2017   J741.5'971   C2016-906236-8

Published in the USA by Drawn & Quarterly,
a client Publisher of Farrar, Straus and Giroux. Orders: 888.330.8477
Published in Canada by Drawn & Quarterly,
a client Publisher of Raincoast Books. Orders: 800.663.5714
Published in the United kingdom by Drawn & Quarterly,
a client Publisher of Publishers Group UK. Orders: info @ pguk.co.uk

Canada Drawn & Quarterly acknowledges the support of the
Government of Canada and the Canada Council for
the Arts for our publishing program, and the National translation program
for Book Publishing, an initiative of the Roadmap for Canada's Official
Languages 2013-2018 : Education, Immigration, Communities, for our
translation activities.

Drawn & Quarterly reconnaît l'aide financière du gouvernement du
Québec par l'entremise de la Société de développement des entreprises
culturelles (SODEC) pour nos activités d'édition. Gouvernement du
Québec—Programme de crédit d'impôt pour l'édition
de livres—Gestion SODEC

Elise Gravel's quirky and charming
characters have won the hearts
of children and adults worldwide,
winning a Governor General's Literacy
Award in 2012 for her book La clé à
molette. She currently has over thirty
children's books to her name, which
have been translated into a dozen
languages. Elise lives in Montreal with
her spouse, two daughters, cats,
and a few spiders.